RETRIBUTION

THE LAZARUS ALLIANCE, BOOK 6

BLAZE WARD

KNOTTED ROAD PRESS

Retribution
The Lazarus Alliance: Book Six
Blaze Ward
Copyright © 2021 Blaze Ward
All rights reserved
Published by Knotted Road Press
www.KnottedRoadPress.com

ISBN: 978-1-64470-205-5

Cover art:
ID 118678447 © Philcold | Dreamstime.com

Cover and interior design copyright © 2021 Knotted Road Press

Reviews
It's true. Reviews help. Even a short one, such as, "Loved it!" So please consider reviewing this book (and all of the ones you've read) on your favorite retailer site.

Never miss a release!
If you'd like to be notified of new releases, sign up for my newsletter.

http://www.blazeward.com/newsletter/

Buy More!
Did you know that you can buy directly from my website?

https://www.blazeward.com/shop/

ALSO BY BLAZE WARD

The Lazarus Alliance

Escape

Return

Rebellion

Revolution

Liberation

Retribution

Alliance

The Jessica Keller Chronicles

Auberon

Queen of the Pirates

Last of the Immortals

Goddess of War

Flight of the Blackbird

The Red Admiral

St. Legier

Winterhome

Petron

CS-405

Queen Anne's Revenge

Packmule

Persephone

Additional Alexandria Station Stories

Siren

Two Bottles of Wine with a War God

The Story Road

The Science Officer Series Season One

The Science Officer

The Mind Field

The Gilded Cage

The Pleasure Dome

The Doomsday Vault

The Last Flagship

The Hammerfield Gambit

The Hammerfield Payoff

The Bryce Connection

The Science Officer Series Season Two

Alien Seas

Shadow of the Dominion

Longshot Hypothesis

Hard Bargain

Outermost

Dominion-427

Phoenix

Princess Rualoh

ONE

LAZARUS

LAZARUS SAT BACK and watched the shattered remains of the latest Innruld Security Pyramid slowly tumbling. Already, escape pods were blasting away from the plasma-streaming wreck, fearful that *Ajax* would continue killing it, but he'd made his point.

Those ships tended to fly point forward, like they were lifting off from the ground of ancient Egypt, so it made it quite easy for Kuei to line them up dead center as they approached, allowing Wybert to harpoon them with the Kirov Lance. One shot, fired right down the exact middle of the ship, annihilating the command section at the tip and then passing down through a variety of engineering spaces underneath.

Lazarus didn't even have to kill that many people to permanently end any given Pyramid as a threat. He did live somewhat in fear of reducing something like this to being no more interesting than killing chickens, but he wasn't there today. Hopefully, none of them would ever get there.

"Sensors," he called out, just to make sure Cormac was listening. "What is their status?"

"*Disabled,*" Cormac replied. "*Possibly terminally although the damage is contained sufficient that they could decide to rebuild this vessel, given time and need.*"

"Do we kill it?" Wybert asked in that high-pitched voice of his that always sounded like a songbird.

"Negative, Fusilier," Lazarus decided. "Pilot, take us into jump someplace else so the station can launch rescue forces."

Kuei acknowledged his order with a flick of her left ear, the inner one as she and Wybert were seated side by side in front of him. She didn't like this any more than he did, but they both had jobs to do if the Species Underground was finally going to be liberated from the Innruld.

That included killing a lot of people, at least until the so-called Masters of the Galaxy decided that they had had enough. Today, that didn't include all of them.

There was a flash of blue light and all the stars around them changed.

"Secure from alert," Lazarus said, containing his sigh inside so he looked and sounded like a commanding officer.

He stood from his command station and stretched. That encounter hadn't even lasted an hour, but *Ajax* could simply step through a hole in space to arrive at optimum range to taunt a Security Pyramid into attacking. This one had been no different. Its fate hadn't been, either.

"All hands stand down for a break rotation," Lazarus ordered. "Cormac, in thirty minutes I want you to turn over operations to an organic assistant so you can join me, Kuei, Wybert, and H'Brige in a meeting."

"*Acknowledged, Captain,*" the NavCrawler said.

Lazarus looked at the other two and got confirmation from them, as well as his Chief Engineer aft, smiling at him from one of the side screens at his station.

In three weeks, his marauders had done an incalculable amount of damage to Innruld control of their own region of space. Revolution would be spreading like wildfire on many worlds.

But all this was just a sideshow.

There was still the war with Westphalia to go fight.

None of this would matter until he resolved those murderers.

TWO

OLUCHI

OLUCHI FOUND himself at something of an impasse, staring across the conference room table at Madam Chera Sonels, leader of the Species Underground on Oton Mari. The Tarni woman was at least smiling. Addison and Admiral da Silva on his side of the table balanced the two of her advisors present as makeweights, but it was really down to just the two of them.

"Why don't you think it will work?" Oluchi asked her.

They'd gone 'round and 'round all morning, but gotten nowhere.

"Without that deadly warship of yours, without *Ajax*, they could just sail in here and retake everything," she replied, leaned back on her abdomen so that her front set of hands could lace fingers across her thorax, just like an accountant, which she was when she wasn't being a revolutionary.

"With what?" Admiral da Silva shifted all his weight forward now.

Sonels rotated her head without moving any other part of

her body. It was weird to look at, but he was the alien here. Him and the other two Humans.

"We've captured and rebuilt three of those Security Pyramids," da Silva continued, reminding her. Again. "At last count Lazarus had destroyed eleven others, and that was before this most current raid. Word will get out, especially as you have sent home all the peons who previously wore an Innruld uniform. Sure, they'll know where you are, but they also know they have nothing that can currently stand against Human technology."

"Until you leave," Sonels retorted tartly. "Until your mighty killer is gone for months on end, leaving us to hang in the wind at the end of a web line."

"I'm not going anywhere," Oluchi reminded her. He gestured at a porthole in the nearby wall. "*Celestial Sovereign* isn't going anywhere, either. I'm not entirely certain that a Security Pyramid is a true threat to that vessel, to say nothing of your three Pyramids here that we are in the process of modifying and upgunning to be more dangerous than any Innruld vessel."

"Mine?" she asked, slightly shocked from the gasp that he heard.

But Oluchi was used to high-stakes poker. Had made a living at it for a long time, as a matter of fact.

"Yours," Oluchi reminded her. "We are here to help you overthrow the Innruld. Not to replace them. The best way to do that is to put the Species Underground in charge of things and then help whenever we can. That means technology transfers, but you don't have the industrial base to build new guns or shield generators. You have what we brought. And we'll bring more, as soon as we can run home."

"Why are you doing this, Pryce?" she asked.

Before he could answer, she gestured at the Admiral on his right and Addison, quietly on his left, both in Rio

Alliance tan uniforms, while he was still in his canary yellow silk. Civilian, through and through.

"And I don't mean the Rio Alliance, or even Yisan, Pryce," she continued. "Why are you, Oluchi Pryce, doing this? What do you expect to gain from it?"

"I'm here because several important people thought that I would be a good candidate to interface with the Species Underground," he said. "Because I know all the key players and have been involved in this almost as long as Addison has. But most importantly because of what's coming."

"And that is?" she asked, as if they hadn't had this conversation any number of times, too, but she was looking for something.

To date, he hadn't been able to find the words that would move her from high center. On the one hand, she'd been living her whole life under the heel of an Innruld boot. They all had. That's what Innruld Space meant, at least to an outsider like him. The so-called Masters of the Galaxy, destined to rule everyone and everywhere.

Right up to the point that they had first encountered the most dangerous, lethal, warlike species ever known. Even an example in a pretty, yellow, silk shirt.

Humans.

He drew a breath and sought a different inspiration. He'd tried patriotism. Appealed to their greed. To their rationality. Everything.

No, only almost everything. Was it finally time to go there?

Oluchi supposed it was.

He turned back from looking out that porthole and studied Chera Sonels's eyes. All of them. It was a spider face, of a sort. Not ugly, nor even unpleasant.

Cold. Calculating. Open to argument, but she hadn't heard the one that would move her.

"Because Westphalia will be here soon," he said simply. "By now they've certainly found the way. When they get here, they'll crush the Innruld even faster and harder than Lazarus has been doing, but there will be a key difference."

"And that is?" she asked, mandibles relaxing now, as if he'd finally gotten her attention.

"They won't stop until they crush all of you."

THREE

EHA

EHA STUDIED the High Councilors around the table. Adriana was asleep in her bassinet along the wall for now, so Eha could concentrate on the nine faces around her. Six Humans, one Gnashiiley, one Moah, and one Atomarsk.

Erlyn Teixeira and Pascia Nkali were each allies in their own way. Chair Cavalcanti wasn't an enemy, so much as a blustery, old fart who still hadn't really wrapped his head around the implications of the future that had arrived when he wasn't looking. Eha wasn't sure any of them really had, but she was forward looking, like a predator, and Cavalcanti was forever looking back over a shoulder like prey.

"You can repair the ship with the facilities at hand?" Eha asked. "It was battered severely by Carlos, but not irreparably?"

"That is correct," Councilor Almeida replied, so Eha turned her attention to him.

Juan Richy Almeida. Human. Male. Past old and approaching elderly now, from the white hair and wrinkled skin. A member of what had been called the Humanist Block on the Council before that new future arrived. The ones that

9

wanted to destroy Westphalia perhaps more than they wanted to help alien refugees.

Sharp. Predatory, but not aimed at her. From what Erlyn had told her, the man was entirely dedicated to ending Westphalia as a threat to the Rio Alliance, which was why he opposed some of the things she had offered or asked for. Fearful, he was, that it would let Westphalia survive one day longer than they should be allowed, and that he might die of old age before he saw the specists on Earth fall from power.

"I would ask what I could do to assist," Eha said to the man. "But we both know that any effort I or my people make would be entirely symbolic at this point, as we are hard at work building our first colony on Liberty."

"We cannot be two places at once," Almeida said. "Nor split our attention to fight a war on two fronts. While I appreciate everything you have done and your flexibility on the topic, I still posit that we would all be better served concentrating all of our efforts on Westphalia. Innruld has been static for centuries. Even a decade more will not change much."

"I agree, Councilor Almeida," Eha replied, listening to the gasps of shock from most of the table.

Not Erlyn, because she and Eha had talked about this ahead of time.

"Further, I think that defeating Westphalia now does the most to protect the innocents of Innruld Space from retribution by either of our enemies," Eha said.

Cavalcanti had learned to gavel quietly enough by now so as to not wake Adriana, and Eha had added some baffling around the sides of her carrier. Not enough to keep a curious kit from poking her head out and perhaps wandering off, but there were Council Aides around the outer edge of the room, ready to run errands as needed. They had all fallen in love with the kit and would watch over her.

But Eha's words still destabilized the room for nearly a minute.

"What are you up to?" Almeida asked now, leaned forward to study her.

"If the captured Westphalian Heavy Starcruiser *Mannheim* can be adequately repaired, it could become a bulwark," Eha said. "If I understand the Human terms, that is. It doesn't have to go anywhere else, but can just sit close to the station and be another defensive gunnery platform, yes?"

More chaos, but politely contained. The lines between Alliance Block and Humanist Block were never rigid, but had ossified somewhat over the years, and were only now breaking down as new formations took hold. New tides threatening.

However, she had just slithered all the way across that gap to plant herself firmly on the other side, and nobody but Erlyn had figured out why. She smiled at all of them.

"You are correct, Madam Dunham," Almeida replied warily. "Why?"

"I have not been privy to any depth of your military history," Eha said. "Nor have I pried, except by reading public histories generally available to all citizens of the Rio Alliance."

The man nodded without speaking.

"Having a second Heavy Starcruiser nearby, plus all the damage that was likely done to the fleet that abandoned it, means that Westphalia is likely back on their coil right now. Rocked onto their heels, I believe would be the Human equivalent."

"That is a safe enough assumption, yes," Almeida replied.

"So the next Humanism would be, if I have it right, striking while the iron is hot," Eha said. "The Rio Alliance has rarely crossed the generally accepted line of demarcation between nations, preferring to fight a defensive war. You've beaten them three times at Vilga's Stand, twice in the last year. That has to sting. Why not attack them right now with *Recife* and part of that squadron? It doesn't have to be anything enormous. Lazarus always talked about using *Ajax* as the galaxy's meanest pirate raider, able to overwhelm and shatter the defensive forces of any planet that didn't have a major fleet protecting it. Why not do that now, while they are off-keel?"

Why not, indeed?

Bedlam this time, but she'd made her point. Cavalcanti would recess to talk, probably until tomorrow at the earliest, so the man could bring in naval leaders and ask them directly, but Eha had spent a lot of time talking to Carlos on the way home. She understood better now folks like Lazarus, who was just the most driven of them, rather than any sort of militaristic aberration.

They would be happy to attack Westphalia.

And thus bring forward the day when the Innruld would fall.

FOUR

GORE

GORE WESCOTT SAT in his private room at the club and tried to absorb the enormity of the latest message from Earth, a highball glass of the good whiskey in one hand almost forgotten because of the piece of paper in the other.

Desperation. That was the only thing he could think of.

Twice in the last two years, the organization he had inherited from his predecessor had come close to being discovered and subsequently destroyed. Pawns had been sacrificed at a master's level, and gone down willingly rather than turn. He and his central group remained, like a worm deep in the guts of Rio's apple.

But now the people in charge on Earth appeared to be getting desperate.

Gore understood that feeling. Messages took months to get to him, unless something was so critical that risks had to jump to unacceptably dangerous levels. What they asked or ordered sometimes had to be ignored because circumstances on the ground had already changed radically.

He was playing chess on a board that kept adding rows

and occasionally even new kinds of pieces subject to alien rules of play.

Alien.

Those damnable aliens had changed the game. Westphalia had been slowly winning, being larger and more aggressive than Rio. The Rio Alliance Navy had taken that huge gamble and built the monstrosity called *Ajax*. Another desperate roll of the dice, but one that had somehow, against all possible odds, succeeded.

Oliveira had found aliens. Been rescued by them. Recruited them. Planted an entire colony of them at Vilga's Stand.

But what was the Rio Alliance, except an expression of those soft-headed fools who thought that all creatures in the galaxy were meant to be equal?

Gore growled quietly to himself and took another sip of his exceptional whiskey before returning to the note in his hand. He let the quick burn of alcohol soothe his nerves and settle him some.

They had lost another battle at Vilga's Stand. That made three now, each of them something that might get its own chapter in a future history of the Rio Alliance. That is, if something wasn't done to destroy everything before all those aliens overwhelmed Humanity and buried it beneath alien germs and diseases.

All men *might be created equal, but not all* beings.

The note did not change on a third reading. Gore could decode it without a cipher key, reading between the lines of an otherwise innocent missive from a distant cousin with whom he appeared to be reasonably-regular pen pals. Words written in ink on paper. Impossible for any sort of electronic surveillance system to monitor and intercept, thereby uncovering his secrets.

Even were they to be read later, the contents meant

nothing to the average reader, and Gore destroyed them all quickly when he was done with them.

Would that he could destroy this one and pretend it had been unseen.

Were they MAD?

But he didn't even allow that question into his eyes, let alone onto his face. Nothing to spoil his countenance and suggest to others that he was anything but a mid-level bureaucrat with an inheritance and a quiet, wealthy lifestyle.

This would shatter his organization, win or lose. They would be a generation rebuilding. If the war was somehow still ongoing long enough because his beloved homeland hadn't been overrun by *ALIENS*.

Gore suspected that the best he could hope for right now was to somehow survive, falling back onto secret identities even his paymasters on Earth were unaware of, so that he could simply vanish, and hopefully escape.

The Rio Alliance would be hunting him with sharpened knives from the instant when he put this plan into action. And he would, as stupid as it was to contemplate.

Those fools on Earth had ordered him to assassinate the Churquen woman. The Ambassador.

Eha Dunham.

FIVE

LAZARUS

LAZARUS LOOKED across the small desk in his office and studied some of his closest friends in the galaxy. Kuei Akeley. Wybert of Capantzina. Cormac the NavCrawler. Grace Savidge.

Vaadwig. Ilount. Computer. Human.

He was only sorry that Addison wasn't here, but they'd see him soon enough and it had indeed been necessary for the man to remain back at Oton Mari, training people and overseeing the repairs to the captured Security Pyramid *Vigilant*.

"We've done what I set out to do," Lazarus told them. "Shattered more Security Pyramids than they probably imagined possible. I have become the single greatest killer in the entire history of the Innruld, though it brings me no pleasure."

"Time for you to go home?" Kuei asked.

She was the quietest of the group, but also generally the leader, when Addison wasn't around.

"Time for *Ajax* to return to Brasilia for repairs and maintenance," he corrected her. "My eventual home is likely to either be someplace like Gowook or aboard some starship for the next twenty years. But *Ajax* needs servicing. And maybe, just maybe, good things have happened while we've been gone."

"Was the force at Vilga's Stand sufficient to hold the system?" Wybert asked, sounding nothing at all like the goofball Ilount who had blown up Lazarus's pincke, way back at the start of all this.

This was a man who would have queens lined up to mate with *him*, as unlikely as that outcome might have seemed two years ago.

"We can only hope," Lazarus nodded. "Carlos is good. *Recife* is a first tier warship. Unless Westphalia sent overwhelming force, that should have been enough. But that unknown is why we cannot go there first. We must find out where things stand, and I can only do that at Brasilia."

"Four weeks home?" Kuei asked. "Or push it and aim for three?"

She smiled, but Akeley's Passage through the Phraettis Nebula was named for her. He'd never known a Pilot with a better instinctive feel for space.

So he smiled wickedly at her. Watched her ears flick backwards slowly as she noted his face and started to grow a little nervous reading him.

"I'd like to do something extravagant," he said, ignoring the other three for a moment.

"How crazy are you getting, Lazarus?" she asked, appetite whetted.

This from a woman who *thrived* on pushing the limits. At least when it came to flying.

"The galaxy is a pancake," he replied, holding up his hands. "From Oton Mari, I'd like you to go something like straight up clear to the edge of open space above or maybe down. Whichever you think is best. Take a second hop straight sideways that just might go into the record books until someone sets out specifically to top you. Then drop down into the Brasilia system in only two or three jumps from there. *Ajax* has the spare power to open those sorts of portals, unlike every other ship I've ever known. Again, a design feature. I'd like to use it. Everybody forgets that we can move faster across physical space compared to anything larger than a Courier when we want to, so I'd like to take advantage of that."

"What happens when we get home?" Grace asked, speaking largely for the others.

"They ordered Rod da Silva to do certain things," Lazarus grinned. "He did, and will be sending me home for more orders and probably requesting back more crew and equipment. Or at least we can aim them towards Oton Mari and let them find their own way here."

"Because you want to go hunting Westphalia," Wybert spoke up now.

Lazarus nodded.

"It is the only way to protect Innruld Space," he replied. "At least until the Species Underground has enough warships with powerful guns to do it themselves. Everything hinges on defeating Westphalia."

"*How much risk does this scenario introduce, Lazarus?*" Cormac spoke up from between Kuei and Wybert.

"I simply cannot calculate it," he replied. "But Eduardo and the elders of Yisan moving closer to Rio puts Westphalia in a bind, as they will have to build forward operating bases deep into the nebula, at least until they figure out how to do what I'm asking of Kuei. Anyone can fly around the shield, but you still have to know what systems you want. Until they find them, we have time."

"Then we shouldn't waste it, should we?" Kuei asked.

He could tell by the way both of her ears were forward

now that she was excited at the prospect, rather than daunted. But then, nothing related to flying ever daunted this woman.

"Any other thoughts?" he asked, but everyone just shook their heads. Or a camera in Cormac's case. "Then, Kuei, I need you to get us back to Oton Mari as fast as possible, so we can put the next leg of things into motion."

They rose excitedly and departed, but Grace remained behind. He smiled at her, but he could tell she had other questions.

"I don't know what Admiral Santos will do," he replied to her unasked question. "Technically, I'm on my third or fourth Court Martial at this point, depending on how you want to interpret things, but right now I'll be working under Rod's orders, so they'll have to listen that much."

"Are they dumb enough to remove you from command?" Grace asked.

"They were dumb enough to put me in command," he retorted with a grin.

"No, that wasn't dumb, Lazarus," she reminded him in her seriousness. "That might have been the single smartest thing they ever did. They will need to remember that."

SIX

AILEEN

AILEEN STUDIED THE GNASHIILEY ADMIRAL, seated behind his desk like battlements to protect him from her. At least the chair she was sitting in today had a space bored through it for her stubby tail.

The Humans were learning.

"You haven't got *anything* better I could use?" she asked, sounding like a teenager forced to go on a long flight with her parents.

Not that she's *ever* been that kid. Honest.

"I do not," Carlos replied, at least taking pains to look embarrassed.

"That ship we brought here just barely flies, you know," Aileen snarked. "I've been on too many Rio ships now to appreciate how badly ours was designed and assembled."

"Understood, Commander, but I need someone to carry these messages to Brasilia," he said. "Someone who understands logistics on both a military and civilian level, because the colony will grow much faster if we can get a couple of freighters' worth of the right basic materials here quickly. Additionally, The Admiralty will want to tear your ship completely apart so they can finally understand what Innruld vessels are like. That means you. And your boyfriend."

"Sidekick," she replied automatically, until she saw his wry grin. Then she shook her head from shoulder to shoulder. "Okay, maybe boyfriend on some future date. I get it. We're all stretched thin, I'm not in your chain of command, and nobody else understands Churquen or Yithadreph. Can I borrow *Mannheim* and haul it to Oton Mari for six months when this is all done?"

"Ask Admiral Santos when you see him," Carlos laughed. "Personally, I'm hoping he leaves *Mannheim* here for a while and sends *Recife* instead. I'd like to be in something with enough guns next time that comes up. *Dutra* was a lovely sailor, but we almost got our tail feathers singed off by a ScoutWall."

"*Dutra* would do as well," she sighed.

"Don't say that too loud, or they might put you in command of her and send you back," he laughed even more.

Aileen couldn't help the shudder. All she'd ever wanted was to play three dimensional puzzles with cargo, packing the most things into the smallest space. Somewhere along the way, she'd turned into Lazarus's second best friend and Second Officer. A Rio Alliance Commander, in spite of not even being Human.

But she had paved the way for whichever numbskulls decided later that they wanted to be warsailors. She'd be fine returning to civilian life.

Unless…

"What?" Carlos asked sharply. "Your eyes just got the most evil smile in them."

"Not *Dutra*," she said. "You and the silly storks ever build armed transports? The big ones, like you use for resupply, but with enough guns on them to handle Westphalian pirates? Or Innruld dipshits?"

"No, but it wouldn't be that hard to add a few guns to a freighter," he replied. "However, you'd probably be better taking something like *Dutra* and hollowing it out even more. That would give you cargo space and speed. Why?"

"*That* might keep me in tan," she laughed with him. "Bigger puzzles than just *Shiva Zephyr Glaive* and her curved cargo space. Anything else will just be boring by comparison."

The admiral smiled and held out a hand across the desk. Aileen shook it.

"I'll send Santos a note and see if they can free up anything, but I promise that I'm recommending you to take command of her if they do," he grinned. "But you have to get that oversized lifeboat to Brasilia first. The primitive technology of that ship will ram it home for Santos and the Council."

"Understood, sir," Aileen said. "We'll get it done."

He nodded, so she rose and exited his office. At least she had Briston with her for this next run. And maybe he was turning into a boyfriend.

She still had to convince the kid to join her in the shower. She hadn't had anyone working the fur on her spine with really good nails since she'd last seen Lazarus and Grace.

SEVEN

OLUCHI

OLUCHI NOTED SARDONICALLY that the galaxy had gone and gotten a lot weirder on him. At least he had Anya, holding his right hand, as he stood here and surveyed the situation. He was with the others on the now-fully repaired bridge of the Freedom Fighter *Vigilant*. No longer an Innruld Security Pyramid, and the Species Underground, for all their decades of Resistance, hadn't yet figured out what kind of government they intended to create.

But then, two years ago, they'd still been trapped beneath an Innruld heel. Until a chance encounter with a couple of smugglers in the middle of nowhere…

However, at the end of the day, Oluchi still hadn't been able to figure out what idiot put him in charge.

After all, Rod da Silva, *ADMIRAL* of the Rio Alliance Navy stood off to one side, while *CAPTAIN* Addison Wolcott was coiled next to the man. Both were deferring to him, as was just about everyone else.

And to top it off, *Ajax* had left a number of bolts of tan fabric behind, so the revolutionaries around him were generally all wearing some uniform in that color, indicating something along the lines of a formal military, if he understood things. Wouldn't stop the Innruld from executing every damned one of them, and him, if they were ever captured, but it turned this from a barroom brawl into a formal thing.

Even an ex-gigolo like Oluchi Pryce could appreciate that.

Anya dropped his hand now and stepped over to stand next to Addison. That left Oluchi alone on this side of the room facing the other two women. Oluchi liked to think of himself as a ladies man, but this was perhaps pushing it. Still, he was surrounded more and more by competent women, so there was always that.

"Madam Sonels," he said formally, nodding to the woman who still led the organization at Oton Mari, before turning to the other woman. "Director Yaaksen."

"Captain," Quija Yaaksen replied. "We'll use Human terms as well, at least as much as possible."

Oluchi shot a glance over at Addison and caught his quick nod, so apparently he'd worked a lot of things out. Oluchi wondered if that included all the training videos that had traveled here with Lazarus and *Ajax*.

Oluchi had seen what those had done to turn Aileen, Kuei, and Wybert into proper officers. And if you needed to create a military from scratch, Oluchi supposed that was a good place to start. Not all of the species were capable of doing violence, and none of them like Humans could.

But what idiot put Oluchi Pryce in charge?

He flipped his opera cape back off one shoulder and focused on CAPTAIN Yaaksen.

She was a Dreeni. For lack of better comparison, she had always struck him as a bipedal hedgehog, covered over with short spines that tended to be blunt, rather than long and spiky like a porcupine. Tan colored all over just a little darker than her uniform, but just barely three and a quarter feet tall. And he was given to understand that females were larger than males.

"Captain," Oluchi replied more carefully, catching a hint of a grin on Chera's mandibles as he did. "I still don't think that I'm the person to be doing this, but welcome aboard *Vigilant*. Under the presumptuous authority of whoever I might represent this week, it is my distinct pleasure to appoint you as commanding officer of this vessel, the first in the Freedom Forces of the Species Underground. You will take command and begin training your crew, subject to appropriate civilian oversight and carry your war to the enemy with honor and dignity."

He'd even helped with the words, but at the end of the day, Oluchi supposed that *civilian* was the key to everything. And why Chera Sonels had wanted him to do it instead of da Silva. The Innruld didn't have a proper military, as a Human might understand the term. They were an enormous gendarme instead.

They didn't have warships either, instead having Security Barcs in a variety of sizes and supposedly several hundred Security Pyramids, but not enough of those to be everywhere.

And that was before Lazarus started blowing them up, anywhere he could find them.

Oluchi held out a hand and Captain Yaaksen reached up to shake it. That was still a new thing to the Species Underground, who were used to bowing to the so-called Masters of the Galaxy. And they still flinched a little whenever they remembered that the movement had evolved among Humans to indicate that they were not holding a weapon in that hand.

Humans, the big, mean, deadly space orcs coming to

overrun the galaxy. Represented by Oluchi Pryce. In canary yellow

"Thank you, Ambassador," Yaaksen replied.

And *that*, he supposed, was what made it all work. He was an Ambassador to the Humans of Yisan, as well as the Rio Alliance. And a civilian. Rod da Silva would be in command at the flotilla level, or even fleet, once they had such a thing, but Quija Yaaksen would command this vessel.

He stepped back and bowed to her now. She did the same and turned to the new command throne that had been installed. Moving to it, she hopped in and powered everything up, telescoping her chair up to the same head height he or Addison would have used.

"All hands, this is your Captain," she said, her voice now booming quietly out of the speaker behind him, and presumably all the way around this enormous flying castle. "We have completed transfer of command and the Freedom Fighter *Vigilant* is now in service. You will continue with your training and duties, and stand by for our first training cruise in three hours."

She cut the line and smiled up at him. Oluchi smiled back. Only then did she turn to da Silva.

"Admiral, what are your orders?" she asked.

Rod stepped forward and came to attention. Like Oluchi, he was playing a role today, but his could get him into all sorts of trouble, considering how far he had stretched some of his orders and interpretations to get here.

Oluchi, at the end of the day, only had to answer to Eduardo Martìnez, and not the entire Rio Alliance Admiralty. As if that made his day of reckoning any less dangerous.

"Captain, let us retire to the primary conference room and have a simple planning session," da Silva replied. "I expect *Ajax* back soon and that starts the next phase of our war."

Yaaksen smiled and lowered her station back down to the point where she could stand. Her legs were even shorter than Aileen's, who called him and the rest of the Humans *storks*. Captain Yaaksen took the lead, setting a sedate pace by Oluchi's standards, but a professional one for Addison, Chera, or Quija Yaaksen.

But Rod had been right. Without *Ajax* in the neighborhood, things were likely to get dangerous.

EIGHT

ADDISON

ADDISON FINALLY FELT the weight slide off his scales, letting his keel flex for the first time in months. Looking around the conference room, he was just an observer today. He nodded silent thanks for that when Rod looked over, catching the twinkle in the man's eyes.

This was just a short vacation for Addison, to be able to go home and see his mate and meet his child. Then he and Lazarus would be back into harness to complete that impossible quest that had begun when a strange vessel first appeared out of nowhere and signaled *Shiva Zephyr Glaive*.

Oluchi was acting like a Chairman of the Board, but he automatically did that when nobody else wanted to step up. The man might not ever realize it. Chera Sonels might have, but she would have to do that more and more starting tomorrow, so maybe she was getting a break this afternoon, too. She'd been right at Addison's side since they took this ship away from the Innruld, including that first battle when it looked like they might all get killed.

Right up to the point *Ajax* stepped in and *Crossed a T*. Quija Yaaksen had impressed Addison with her ability to transform from a semi-retired director with experience on cruise ships into a war-fighter, and she would need that, but she also had Rod as an admiral, so all she had to do was command her ship and let him fight the war around her.

Until Westphalia got here, there was nothing the Innruld had that could take on three Pyramids at once, now that the other two were almost repaired and upgraded.

Now, Addison just had to find a way to prevent Admiral da Silva from somehow promoting him to Rear Admiral and putting him in charge of the Revolutionary Navy or Freedom Forces. Whatever it ended being called. Rod and Lazarus had always been adamant that the War of Liberation would have to be led by the Species Underground. Humans could and would help, but the one thing Lazarus had demanded of Addison, in private, was that there would be an alliance. Not just the Rio Alliance *Expanded*, but Rio would ally with Yisan and the Species Underground as equal partners.

Three friends fighting two common enemies for the future of the galaxy. Simple, right?

"I suppose this meeting will come to order," Oluchi announced in an off-hand way, leaning forward to put his elbows on the table and then rest his chin on his fists. He needed to remind everyone that this was a civilian thing, so he didn't want to look like Lazarus always did. "First order of business has been completed, with command of *Vigilant* turned formally over to the Species Underground. Madam Sonels?"

"It is a start," she replied. "Our three former Pyramids are sufficient to take on four or maybe five of theirs, if they ever assemble such a force again. And messages have been sent to other systems, both to recruit more sailors and to activate other cells. You will understand that many people will hear the news and discount it as an impossibility."

Addison nodded and smiled.

"You will find yourself using that phrase many times, when discussing Lazarus," he said. "I know I have."

"So we have planned and worked for many lifetimes," Sonels said now with a sharp nod. "The time has arrived to decide what it is we wish to make of ourselves. Captain Wolcott, what would you contribute to the discussion before you take a leave of absence?"

Addison drew a breath to the tip of his tail and pulled everything close before he spoke.

"I do not believe that my opinion is the best one, Chera," he said simply, waving a hand to interrupt when she started to reply. "If it was left to my discretion, the Innruld would be ended as a species entirely. Not just broken, but destroyed. Hunted down to the last kit. But I understand that this will not be a popular opinion, at least among a significant slice of the population. Others will be one hundred percent behind me. I know this from my many years as a smuggler delivering all manner of prohibited substances specifically designed to cause lethargy among that species, that they might slowly breed themselves out of existence."

Addison leaned back and studied the woman. Yaaksen was taking Addison's place in their chain of command, so he didn't know what the leaders would do with him when he got back, unless he was supposed to replace Rod. Or worse, Rod might be sending messages to Brasilia requesting that the Admiralty place Addison in command of a proper Rio warship. Not another *Ajax*, but even a Light Starcruiser could destroy anything less than a Pyramid easily. And maybe slug it out with one of those monsters and win, depending.

He just wanted to see Eha, but he also knew that he hadn't given everything to the cause that he could. It might be another decade before he was free. Assuming Westphalia could be defeated.

There was always that secondary mission to just send

colony ships into the dark. The Humans might not understand it, but the Churquen and the Yithadreph would scatter like seedpods if the Innruld blinked long enough.

If Rio lost, he could rescue his family and vanish.

Assuming he survived.

"Captain, I might remind you that xenocide is contrary to the rule of the Rio Alliance Navy," da Silva spoke up in a carefully neutral tone.

"This is no longer about Rio, Rod," Addison replied, addressing the man informally by his name and not his rank. "This is how the Species Underground decides that they will handle their former slave masters. You may advise, but not dictate. If those actions require me to remove the tan uniform permanently, I will do so in a heartbeat. You know that."

"I do," da Silva nodded sagely. "This is to remind you that it may not be necessary, once they are broken, just as we will not ever hunt down and destroy every Human who ever served Westphalia. To remind you that certain actions need to be measured in generations or even centuries hence, when we are all gone save for certain history books who will portray us as heroes or villains."

Addison hated it when the man was right, but he was. He flashed back to a conversation with Cormac, away now on *Ajax* hunting, where the two of them might have to ask themselves what Eha would have done, since they both knew their own minds. He amended that to Eha and Chera now.

"I will see the Innruld broken," Addison growled.

"And I will help," Rod assured him. "But we will do it like *professionals*."

Addison couldn't help his shudder, but the civilians in the room—which was everyone else—didn't automatically understand professionalism as da Silva used the term.

Professionals in the Rio Alliance Navy, willing to do unmitigated violence to total strangers at the drop of a hat.

And smile doing it.

"We will," Addison promised, wondering if someone might yet *order* him to commit xenocide.

He doubted that there were many people Chera could give such orders to. At least yet.

Chera Sonels had watched the byplay subside and turned to him now.

"What will the Innruld do?" she asked. "You have taken Oton Mari. You have captured three Pyramids, and destroyed perhaps a dozen others. Vast swaths of Innruld Space cannot be adequately supervised, as they might see it. How will they react?"

Addison wondered why the woman bothered to ask him, but nobody else here had the experience. Rod was military to the bone, but only Human. The others had never commanded warships in battle.

Addison Wolcott, Revolutionary Captain. Churquen Statesman? He shuddered, but only inside.

"Given enough time, they will regain their equilibrium," Addison decided. "Someone in Innruld itself will decide to gather up a force for the ages and throw it at us here. Perhaps a dozen or even a score of Pyramids next time."

The gasps around the table told him how small some of these people had been dreaming, while he had lain awake at night coming up with scenarios, so he could prepare for them, at least emotionally.

"Can we stop that?" Yaaksen asked.

"No," Addison replied simply. "We cannot, with anything less than *Ajax*, and perhaps not even then, depending on how desperate they get."

"Desperate, Captain?" Chera asked now.

"What happens if an Innruld Pyramid decides to sacrifice

itself and rams *Vigilant* in battle?" he countered. "Even the wreckage might destroy us, if Captain Yaaksen shattered it with guns beforehand. They win a war of attrition that way."

"Your suggestion?" she pressed.

"Fan the flames of revolution," Addison decided. "Understand that people will get killed, and order them to begin sabotaging the Innruld and their lackeys at every turn. If they cannot turn their backs on the systems they are currently holding, they cannot withdraw enough forces to attack us here."

Her eyes got big, but he wasn't done.

"Then take every ship you can arm, and assemble them into swarms like hungry insects, and throw them at system after system," Addison continued. "If you destroy or capture every Security Barc in their inventory, they lose control of every system. That cascades outward. That brings the Innruld down. Pyramids are only good in one system at a time, so there are ten or fourteen other systems with only Barcs holding the chains. Break those."

He turned to da Silva.

"Would the Admiralty send us a protector squadron?" he asked his superior officer. "*PL-371* and her cohorts by themselves could clear any system of Barcs, while outrunning any Pyramid in existence. Throw in local armed freighters and that's your war won, right there."

"I will ask, Captain," Rod said. "No promises, but gunboats are cheaper than Heavy Starcruisers and they might go for that. Pity we sent that ScoutWall home. I could have used them right now."

Addison nodded. Those five ships could have scoured most of Innruld Space clean of Innruld.

And all their lackeys.

Yes, he needed to have a conversation with Admiral Santos when he got to Brasilia.

NINE

ERLYN

ERLYN HAD BEEN a High Councilor for many years. She was used to seeing things evolve with the speed of bureaucracy so she was pleasantly shocked to see her other Councilors suddenly breaking out of their old modes of thinking. It was even possible that the old schism between Alliance Block and Humanist Block, as polite as it had been, might break down entirely now.

As the ancient saying went: *Nothing like a good hanging to focus the mind.*

She and Eha were having dinner this evening in Erlyn's apartment in the government palace. Adriana had a babysitter for the night, so the two of them could talk, and they were alone once the chef had withdrawn. Dinner had been divine, and they were enjoying a decaf tea while making small talk.

The knock at the door was unexpected. Erlyn opened it to discover Pascia standing there. Erlyn smiled at her.

"Should I worry?" Erlyn asked, just the slightest bit sarcastically as she opened the door and stepped back, inviting the woman in with one hand.

"Hire better spies, maybe," Pascia replied with a grin. "Eha."

"Pascia."

They all ended up in the living room. Eha had a pillow permanently there, with Erlyn on the couch and Pascia in a wingback chair.

"To what do I—we—owe the pleasure?" she asked.

"I can't just swing by in a neighborly fashion?" Pascia asked, mock hurt on her face, but Erlyn wasn't the least bit fooled.

She'd known the Councilor for too many years.

"Would you like to sell me a bridge?" Erlyn countered.

Pascia just laughed.

"I'm here because Juan didn't think it appropriate for him to be seen calling on you this late in the evening," she grinned. "Something about that being how rumors started."

Another round of laughs. Councilor Juan Almeida was nobody's idea of a stud. Oluchi, now, that might have started tongues to wagging.

"So what message did Juan want to pass, that the teacher didn't catch all of us out?" Erlyn asked.

She still had her moments when she refused to act like a grownup. Too many adults had forgotten how to have fun along the way.

Pascia sobered. The room seemed filled with a sudden chill.

"He thinks that Eha is correct about Westphalia perhaps getting a little desperate," she said. "It would not do to suggest that she wasn't safe, here at the very core of the Rio Alliance government, but the word he used was irreplaceable."

"Me?" Eha gasped. "How?"

"You are the bridge to Lazarus," Pascia said.

Erlyn grinned at the term, but only on the inside.

Nobody ever called him Captain *Pancho* Oliveira anymore. Only Lazarus.

"In addition to that, you are the connection to Addison," Pascia continued. "And the colonists at Liberty. And any number of other things. We need to protect you, even more than any of us."

Erlyn sobered. Pascia and Juan had hit on perhaps a wrinkle nobody had truly appreciated, at least until it was spelled out like that. Eha Dunham really was the hinge around which everything revolved going forward. Oluchi Pryce had done well, pretending to replace her while she'd been gone, but Erlyn had thought at the time that the man was just letting his ego get the better of him. It turned out that she owed him an apology, the next time they were together.

He had been trying to be Eha while she was gone.

"Shit," Erlyn muttered.

Pascia nodded. Eha's scales flared around her eyes and her tail thwapped the pillow once hard enough to indicate her emotional state.

"This is not the first time," Eha surprised her by announcing. "Risk, that is. You forget how many years I was a spy and runner, back at places like Aceanx or Zhoonarrim. Does Councilor Almeida have any suggestions for how my security might be improved over what I already have?"

"I suggested a bodyguard or three, but he just laughed in my face," Pascia replied.

"Really?" Erlyn gasped, sorry she'd missed that dour man experiencing public mirth. It might have been decades since that had happened. "What, then?"

"Juan suggested she would be safest someplace like *Recife*, out at Liberty, with another small fleet protecting her," Pascia said. It didn't come across as levity. "Have Carlos Nguema protecting her like he is the colonists, but

39

from aboard the ship itself, where she could flee if she had to."

"You're serious," Erlyn whispered. "He's serious."

"He is," Pascia replied before turning to Eha. "This is not some scheme on his part to separate you from the rest of the High Council, either, my dear. He has taken your words to heart and has begun to bend the ear of Admiral Santos and the Admiralty. He sees you as the symbol that might just rally the entirety of Rio to that mission, like a Grail Quest or something."

Eha nodded. She licked her lips once, looking nothing like a snake when she did that so much as nervous, Human woman.

"The single safest place in the galaxy for me would be aboard *Ajax*," she said after a moment. "*Recife* would be a good second, but only a second. And then not if you were serious about sending him on an expedition into Westphalian space."

"Understood," Pascia nodded. "Perhaps *Mannheim*, if they intend to repair it and leave it there to anchor that system's forces. But I wanted to sound you out, because Juan is serious about demanding that we take some of those ships freed up from piracy patrol near Yisan and use them quickly, before Westphalia understands what we're up to. Eha, would you be amenable?"

"Pascia, perhaps it would be useful if the Council sent an official delegation to Liberty?" Erlyn interrupted. "A fact-finding mission, as it were. You and me, escorted by Eha and Adriana. Obviously, Santos would have to send a major fleet to protect us, over and above what's there. That's too tempting a target, if the word got out."

Pascia turned to her now, eyes appraising.

"Two birds, one stone, Erlyn?" she asked.

"Five or six, if you want to be technical about it," Erlyn

replied with a grin. "Plus, that lets Santos organize an assault from Vilga's stand by pulling in all those ships and rearranging them when nobody is looking. They can go straight at some Westphalian system, while you and I can see how the colony is coming along, thoroughly protected overhead. Eha is safe with us. The Council shows that it cares about the refugees. I see that as a major public relations win, all the way across the board. Eha?"

She turned to the object of their discussion. Erlyn had to remember that Eha had lived a much more dangerous life than anyone even remotely associated with the High Council. Only Admiral Santos had probably been threatened with death as many times as a spy like Eha Dunham.

"Yes," Eha said simply, nodding. "I like it, and it serves many different needs simultaneously. Will the rest of the Council go for it?"

"Quietly, I suspect six votes without twisting any arms at all," Pascia said. "The Humanist Block wants to defeat Westphalia, and this plays into that need. The Alliance Block wants to protect the colonists and expand the Alliance. Hell, Roald might be looking at eight votes in favor before he realizes that it was a done deal, if nobody leaks to him."

Erlyn chuckled. Roald didn't get rolled very often, but this might be the one.

Plus, it would be nice to see Alla and the others again.

Especially if they had to start seriously worrying about assassins in the night.

TEN

AILEEN

AILEEN STILL DIDN'T LIKE the damned old ship, but it had gotten her here. The ancient thing hadn't even broken down more than twice, which was better than *Shiva Zephyr Glaive* would have done over a similar distance. And Briston had repaired it just fine both times.

He was even beginning to relax around her, but Aileen had stopped short of asking if he'd want to scrub her back. That could wait until they got somewhere, rather than being trapped in a broken-down freighter for weeks.

But they'd made it to Brasilia. Gone through all that stupid rigmarole with being an alien ship in the inbound lane, sent off to one side and surrounded by guns and marines.

Aileen looked out the front portal and watched the Rio Alliance monster *Curitiba* drift carefully closer. Another Heavy Starcruiser, like *Recife*. They couldn't dock with this wreck, so a shuttle was coming across the gap for them. Big one, too, rather than the wee pincke she'd been expecting.

"Briston, company will be docking in three minutes," she

announced over the intercom. "Put everything on standby until they tell us what's up and meet me at the airlock."

"Yes, ma'am," he replied.

Aileen already had her bag packed and waiting next to the airlock. His was there as well. She could step right off this tub and let them turn it into target practice, for all she cared. Lazarus really had spoiled her for proper Rio Navy hardware, so she didn't think she'd ever be able to go back to something like *Shiva Zephyr Glaive*. Not that Eha would let Addison do so either, so maybe they'd have to blackmail the Navy into giving them something nice to fly when they retired.

She shut everything down and headed aft as the first thumps of contact jarred the ship. The airlock was beeping when she got there, so whoever was on the other side was either in a hurry, or that good. Briston was just barely next to her by the time the door finished opening.

"Commander Enjehn?" a young lieutenant was standing there in boarding armor, his rank painted in the center of his chest.

"Correct," she replied.

A mob swarmed out of the shuttle, sliding by her and headed all directions.

"What the hell is that?" she demanded, maybe a little sore, but dealing with the storks again had rubbed her a little wrong.

"We've been ordered to take this ship into drydock after you depart, sir," the man replied. "This is a replacement crew so that you can get to Admiral Santos immediately."

Worse, he saluted. She returned it, thankful that she hadn't put Briston in tan for any of this, so he could see it as an outsider and only then decide if he wanted to do something so stupid as take an oath.

Aileen shouldered her pack and studied the helpful stork.

It felt like things had just gotten weird again.

AILEEN JUST WATCHED ADMIRAL SANTOS, seated at the center of four more such illustrious creatures that she was certain they expected her to genuflect before them, or something.

"That's…one hell of an interesting report, Commander," Santos finally replied as he digested the executive summary she'd delivered. They still had to wade through a crap ton of reports, but the Rio Alliance Navy seemed to operate on the mass of paperwork that they generated each and every day. She'd kept good records as Quartermaster, but these people were nuts.

"Commander, what is your recommendation at this point?" one of the goobers on her right asked.

Older Human male. Like ancient in ways that she couldn't identify right off-hand.

"That's up to Admiral da Silva, Admiral Nguema, and Lazarus," she replied. "I got sent by everyone because they all need supplies and I do that better than anyone you have."

Okay, maybe bragging a little, but she'd been talking for two hours now, and her jaw and her tail hurt because she was sitting in a stupid, Human chair again.

Santos got a gleam in his eyes that she didn't trust one damned bit.

"Good news, Commander," he said. "We were already planning to send a force to Liberty, so you'll be able to work with their logistics teams to update everything Carlos needs. And I note that you and Carlos had a conversation about armed cargo transports capable of making the long run to…"

He stopped there and rifled through the papers in front of him for a moment.

"What is the closest system through Akeley's Passage?" he asked. "Dormell or Aceanx?"

"Probably still Zhoonarrim, sir," Aileen replied with a shrug. "Straight shot from the mouth of the nebula for a ship with stardrives, even though it is farther away in trans-space."

"We will need to send such ships to Oton Mari, Commander," Santos smiled at her in a way that felt like she was about to get the shaft, but Aileen didn't flinch, even so much as her ears. "The Admiralty had been assembling such a force, but that got put a little on the back burner over the last month as other things came up. You'd like to be back to *Ajax* as soon as possible, correct?"

She nodded, unhappy with it already, *whatever* it was.

"I'm the Second Officer on that vessel, sir," she reminded him, wondering if that would matter squat to the Human. "It will be good to be home."

The four stranger admirals all stirred at her choice of words, but Aileen had said it automatically. *Ajax* was home to her, at least until everyone found a new ship and they could go back to just running cargo.

Legitimate cargo, even.

"So you might not appreciate your own command, Enjehn?" he asked tentatively.

"That is correct, sir," she said.

Based on conversations with Lazarus, the further stir among those old birds wasn't surprising. Every one of them had fought tooth and nail for an independent command, and then had to be pried out of that command station later.

Not her style.

"There is a rarely-used rank, Commander Enjehn," Santos said. "*Commodore*. Usually, it is applied to the senior captain in a squadron of similar vessels, just so one of them is in command over their nominal peers."

Aileen nodded warily.

"The four vessels we're planning to send to Oton Mari, now that we've reviewed your records, all have commanders in charge. Rather than promote you to captain, and thus make it difficult for you to return to your duties with Lazarus, we propose sending you as a Commander/Commodore, with those four ships under your authority until you can get them to Admiral da Silva and the Species Underground, at which time you will revert to Second Officer and do whatever Rod and Lazarus need. How does that sound?"

"About as good as I could have hoped for, sir," Aileen replied.

Honest words, however sarcastic in her mind. Better than she'd feared, but everyone had warned her that she would be wild-carding this.

At least she'd be home soon.

If she was lucky.

ELEVEN

LAZARUS

IT WAS the dark of evening. Lazarus had turned the lights down enough to sleep, but was too wound up to relax, even wrapped around Grace's form, with only two T-shirts between flesh. But she was awake, too. She rolled to face him.

"Can't sleep?" she asked, one finger reaching up and tracing a line on his cheek.

"We'll be there tomorrow," he said.

"And everything changes," she nodded.

He nodded as well.

"We'll need a week or two in drydock at a dead minimum, just assuming all the parts we need were stockpiled ahead of time," he said. "I've probably already shaved five or ten years off the expected lifespan of this ship, but we've seen more combat in the last two years that I expected in ten. And then I get to deal with the Admiralty."

"Will they be that bad?" she asked.

Lazarus had to stop and remember that this woman had never been in a military. Her deadliness had come from other places, and Eduardo had hired her directly.

"I'm doing what Rod ordered," he said. "But only after going absent once and ignoring orders to return *Ajax* to the fold. They will be in complete control tomorrow, and owe me at least one Court Martial. It might be all over tomorrow."

"Santos does not strike me as a moron, Lazarus," Grace smiled, lifting a huge weight off his shoulders just like that. "But we'll face it together."

"They might arrest me and deport you," Lazarus reminded her.

"Then I'd have to perhaps go to Yisan and recruit a couple of friends to help rescue you," she turned serious, even while smiling. "I might have even done that once. I don't think that Rio appreciates that you can destroy the Innruld by yourself, if Yisan put some effort behind you. Eduardo would do that. You have options."

All he'd ever wanted was to design a better starship. But she was right. He would go back to Oton Mari any way he could, either leading a fleet or sneaking aboard a stolen freighter, and help them.

The Innruld were already swaying heavily in that wind he'd summoned.

It wouldn't take much to push them over.

But he still had Westphalia to face.

TWELVE

PEDRO

ADMIRAL PEDRO SANTOS didn't get to throw his weight around often. The Rio Alliance Navy was a bureaucratic beast at the best of times, and officers like Rod da Silva and Carlos Nguema had pushed the margins quite a bit, even before a top secret weapons research project suffered what should have been a catastrophic failure, before instead accidentally turning the entire galaxy on its head.

However, he threw his weight around when *Ajax* appeared in the inbound lane. Immediately ordered them to come to drydock in the same space where Enjehn's little freighter was being dismantled, because that one had been reserved for *Ajax* first anyway, so it had otherwise been kept empty.

He turned to smile at the various women standing next to him on the dock as they all watched that graceful killing machine get nosed slowly into dock by a series of tugs; High Councilors Teixeira and Nkali, plus Ambassador Dunham and her daughter, who perked up out of her basket to watch through the big picture window. Even Commodore Enjehn was present.

Teixeira was studying him sidelong, so she stepped around everyone and gestured him towards a quiet corner. Several marines shuffled away as they approached.

"What are you up to, Admiral Santos?" she murmured. "This all feels sudden."

"I was sending you and a flotilla to Liberty, as suggested," he smiled savagely at her. "Plus a Consular Mission, so extra ships. Aileen will be along with two ships of supplies for the colony and four ships for Oton Mari. Plus a couple of escorts against piracy. And then Lazarus returned like the Prodigal Son."

She paused, looking up at him with perhaps a hint of fear in her eyes, but Teixeira was a civilian, at the end of the day, and Pedro doubted that they were nearly as superstitious as sailors got.

"What am I missing?" she asked.

Pedro smiled. At least she was smart enough to catch on.

"*Ajax* was designed to kill enemy Starcruisers, Councilor," he noted, indicating that beautiful ship with the tilt of his head. "Not swarms of GunWalls, mind you, although Commander Wolcott has taught us a new maneuver likely to be named after him for that scenario. You and the Council wanted a strike into Westphalian Space, to remind those villains that we can also attack, as infrequently as we do. Lazarus of Bethany will hold that harpoon in his hand."

"And then what?" she asked carefully.

Ah, good. The woman had realized that the *obvious* wasn't *sufficient*.

"Those two escorts I'm sending with Aileen are old and deficient, in any battle on this side of the Nebula, Councilor," Pedro smiled. "The four freighters are loaded up with guns, generators, shield systems, and tools for making the same. We'll turn it all over to Oluchi Pryce for whoever is in charge over there. A bribe, Councilor, but a necessary one, as everyone else has moved faster than we have, and we need to buy our way back into the good graces of those folks over there. Plus, if they can resist a few Westphalian probes, that turns Earth's attention to the interior. *Ajax* may or may not stay in concert with Admiral Nguema after a hard forward raid, but *Ajax* alone will chill those folks on Earth."

"To what end?" she pressed.

"That thing we've dedicated our careers and our lives to, Councilor Teixeira," Pedro said in a hard voice. "Victory over Westphalia. Now we have the chance to lead a grand alliance of dozens of species doing it, and not just the ones that currently make up the Rio Alliance."

Beeping interrupted any conversation as the airlock tunnel extended and mated with the side of the ship.

"Your pardon, Councilor," Pedro nodded and started to walk away from her. "I need to be first down that tunnel."

The others made way, although Eha was right behind him as he got there, not that he or anyone would dispute that woman's place.

The inner hatch finally opened and Lt. Lam stood at attention. Pedro grinned when the man recognized him with a gasp and a whitening face. Technically, Lam was also up for a Court Martial, after the second battle at Vilga's Stand. The sudden terror in the man's eyes reflected that.

"***Admiral on the deck!***" he yelled, snapping hard to attention and turning ninety degrees away.

Pedro nodded at him and looked past the man.

Lazarus and Addison both wore Captain's rank now, but he'd known that was coming from Rod's reports. Good.

He stepped to that red line in the deck and carefully stopped.

"Permission to come aboard, Captain?" he asked in a voice that probably sounded too merry, when everyone around him was used to the serious man the job required him to be.

He saluted both of them, as well as everyone else in the chamber. It felt good.

"Permission granted, sir," Lazarus returned the salute. "Welcome aboard."

Pedro stepped across, and then immediately to his left, out of the way.

"Captain Wolcott, we brought you a surprise."

And everything went to hell as Eha and Adriana were right there.

It felt really good to be able to do that one good thing.

Tomorrow was going to be rough.

THIRTEEN

LAZARUS

LAZARUS HAD everyone in the biggest conference room for what he could only call a war council. Technically, Admiral Santos was in charge, seated at the end of the table. Lazarus had Eha and the cute kit Adriana next to him and Addison beyond that. Two High Councilors were present, although he did know Teixeira reasonably well and Eha liked the woman.

And he had Aileen back, finally. Lazarus hadn't appreciated how much not having her aboard had weighed on his soul. She was next to Grace, with Kuei and Wybert.

Lazarus felt the future tapping on his shoulder as Admiral Santos finally cleared his throat. Adriana was coiled about her mother's arm, studying this stranger who was smiling at her as Addison finally got to meet his own future.

"Clear the room," Santos said to the ubiquitous marines that followed him everywhere. "Lam, you stay."

Ajax didn't have enough crew members to need security marines, and had never had a full crew at all, since sailing on that first mission to test everything and running into a trap.

Santos waited until the door was closed and locked. He

took a breath and looked around the room, finally turning serious again. For the last several hours, it had been like a stranger had taken over his flesh from the man Lazarus had seen before.

"This meeting will come to order," he said simply.

It was like someone had pulled a plug and drained every drop of frivolity out of the room. He turned towards Lazarus.

"Captain Oliveira," he nodded and paused. "Lazarus, these plans were already in motion when you arrived, so I'm not going to do anything except delay for two weeks, or however long you'll need. We've ordered you up more crew members, and those folks will be assembling as quickly as the Bureau of Personnel can organize them, but you were down the list and I have been sending folks to Liberty and preparing for a long haul to Oton Mari with Commodore Enjehn."

Lazarus smiled and caught Aileen's grimace. She'd hate every second of it, but would do it because it got her that much closer to being back in banana-colored capris and her favorite maroon vest.

"Sir," Lazarus replied mostly as a placeholder.

"We're playing an elaborate shell game, Lazarus," Santos continued. "Two High Councilors are headed on a fact-finding mission to Liberty. I'm sending a fleet to protect them, along with supplies, and a convoy that will continue outwards from there."

Lazarus nodded. He'd gotten the gist of that.

"As you are currently attached to Admiral da Silva's mission, I am not detaching you from that, Lazarus," he smiled now. "But I will borrow you for a short period of time. Namely, you will accompany Admiral Nguema when he goes to hit the planet Esmer, in the 6422 Librae system. His was intended to be merely a demonstration raid, more than anything, but *Ajax* changes my calculus."

Lazarus smiled now.

"Admiral, what exactly do you mean by a demonstration raid?" Erlyn Teixeira asked in a cautious tone from nearby.

"A fleet consisting of a number of Heavy and Light Starcruisers, Councilor, with escorts," the man replied. "They drop down into the system and if the defending forces are outnumbered or badly arrayed, they attack. If too strong, then Admiral Nguema is seen, and that makes the other side nervous. We're not trying to hold the system or conquer the planet Esmer. Just to get someone's attention."

"And *Ajax*?" she pressed.

"He can do things that the Westphalian fleet is not prepared to counter at present, madam," Santos actually smiled at her, which might have been a first, as far as Lazarus knew. "If the situation warrants, I expect Nguema to go after enemy Heavy Starcruisers with the intent of damaging or killing as many of them as possible. They lost *Mannheim* to us and *Gotland* only barely escaped with their lives. *Ajax* will greatly play on their nerves when they recognize her."

"And after Esmer, Admiral?" Lazarus spoke up now.

Pedro Santos studied him for a long moment.

"Rod da Silva wants you back," the man replied. "Presumably to kill more Security Pyramids and help expand that war. I am not going to give you orders you might not follow, Lazarus, so I will trust your judgment that you won't leave Carlos in a bad spot. However, I will remind you that we won't win the war in Innruld Space, as much as you might want to try. Nor will we lose it there, regardless of what some people might say. We win it when Earth surrenders. Not until then."

"But they will try to take Innruld Space, Admiral," Lazarus said.

"And hopefully that mistake will bleed them dry, Captain," the man turned even more serious. "Wellington and the Peninsular Campaign. Napoleon in Imperial Russia. Nimitz and the Pacific Campaign. I appreciate that your orders and your loyalties might be at odds right now, but if you do end up at Oton Mari, or wherever Pryce and da Silva are, keep that in mind."

FOURTEEN

GORE

IT WASN'T his wonderfully homey Club. At this point, Gore was certain that he could never set foot in there, ever again. Sad, but being caught and thrown in prison was worse, and he had enough money stashed away to hide forever.

No, he'd simply coughed a tremendous amount one afternoon at work, until everyone told him to go home and see a doctor. Then walked out the door, grabbed a bag at home, and changed identity papers. Gone, never to be seen again.

There was nobody who would raise an alarm until he went missing for a few days. Worse, his housekeeper Berka, presumably the assassin that Westphalia had sent to keep watch over him, was dead and out of his way.

Tragic accident. Of a certainty.

He stood at the edge of a park and watched foot and vehicle traffic across the street. The afternoon was crisp and a little blustery, but the walk here from his new motel had done him good. The pedestrians around the area ignored him and went about their mid-morning business.

Gore waited until he saw his target approach, and then watched the man slip into the coffee and pastry shop across the street. Nobody seemed to be following him, but Gore waited for several minutes anyway.

Finally, it was time. He crossed carefully at the intersection and let the smell of freshly fried donuts draw him into the place. It was not the smell of his childhood, as Gore had grown up in an upper class household with a full staff, and a family chef who would have never stooped to *donuts*.

But at the same time, the smell brought Gore a sense of solace. He'd been planning on just a cup of their barely-burned-sufficiently coffee, but he found himself wandering in front of the display case, almost like a child sticking his nose against it.

The young woman on the far side smiled indulgently.

"A size two vanilla chai latte," he said, finally standing up. "And one of those cinnamon rolls with half chocolate and half caramel frosting."

"Would you like it warmed?" she asked helpfully.

Gore considered it, and nodded.

It would be a hot mess to eat, but didn't that describe, well, *everything?*

He paid and took his prize to the table where Benedict Spearing sat. Along with a fork and many, many napkins.

It was unfortunate that they had to meet in public, as someone knowing Spearing might somehow recognize Gore in his new disguise, but it could not be helped. The shop was large, but nearly empty at this time of morning, save for an *au pair* with a pair of well-behaved four-year-old twins, clear across the way. They weren't making much noise, but it would still mask his conversation from casual listeners.

Gore sat and spent several moments arranging things.

The smell of sugar and confections had bored into his brain now, and he *needed* a bite of the roll before anything else.

Last supper for the condemned, perhaps, and all that?

Spearing sipped his coffee and ruminated on whatever deep-cover spies like that man did when their entire careers teetered on the brink of failure for reasons entirely outside their control.

It was a feeling Gore knew well.

Finally, Gore looked up, chewing contentedly and letting the pastry melt into that hollow spot that had somehow appeared in his soul.

"What news?" he asked innocently, gauging the man's tells and tendencies.

"There have been no leaks," Spearing replied quietly before amending himself. "As yet. Our careful plans may have been blown asunder by the rawest of bad luck."

Gore groaned quietly and sipped to wash his palate clean. "What now?"

"*Ajax* has returned to Brasilia, bearing both Oliveira and Wolcott," Spearing replied. "The ship immediately went into orbital drydock and my sources report that Admiral Santos went aboard, along with two High Councilors and Ambassador Dunham."

"And *Curitiba*?" Gore pressed.

"We have an agent aboard that vessel," Spearing nodded. "A true patriot willing to sacrifice himself to accomplish his mission. However, I would suggest that it is unlikely that Dunham will be transported aboard the Heavy Starcruiser if *Ajax* and her mate are here."

"Last time, they set off for Vilga with barely enough crew members to fight the ship," Gore remembered. "What is their status now? Could we get that agent transferred? Or send a second one aboard *Ajax*?"

Spearing drew a heavy breath before he spoke.

"That will leave fingerprints everywhere, sir," he replied. "The entire organization will be uncovered, arrested, and destroyed, if either agent is successful or not."

Gore nodded. Grimaced.

"Those were the orders from home, Spearing," he retorted, angry at himself rather than this agent. "Those were the costs they expected us to pay. Order it and then activate your contingencies now, so that you have that much of a head start."

"And you?"

"Gore Wescott is already dead," he replied. "Sometime in the next few days, someone will find evidence of a struggle in his luxury suite, followed by several brutal murders and a ransom note that will lead them absolutely nowhere."

"I see," Spearing recoiled, the hand holding his coffee suddenly jittery.

"In fact, this is the last time you and I will meet," Gore continued. "You have your orders, which include taking any risk possible to assassinate the woman. That includes, per our Earth masters, destroying the entire organization in the process. Once you send your orders, I suggest you run for your life, and hope that you can make it to safe space before a warrant catches up with you."

"Is it that desperate?" Spearing gasped.

"It was that desperate when Dunham arrived and first began talking to the High Council, Spearing," Gore replied. "Since then, it has only gotten worse."

FIFTEEN

OLUCHI

OLUCHI HAD SOMEHOW BEEN BLACKMAILED into yet another stupid idea, but this one didn't surprise him one damned bit. And the Admiral could be quite convincing when he wanted to. And as with many other things around here, he was the only person capable of handling this task properly.

At least he'd convinced Anya to accompany him, when Rod da Silva had *somehow* talked Antonia into taking *Celestial Sovereign* on a raiding patrol around nearby Innruld Space.

He was on the bridge now, carefully out of Antonia's way as she and her crew worked, with Anya next to him holding his hand and basically keeping him from shivering with fear or anticipation. It was hard to tell them apart.

"Passive sensors detect no Innruld Pyramids down near the station, Captain," a woman called from where she was face-down over a big screen, reading her esoteric incantations.

"Anything interesting?" Antonia replied, seated at her command station like a proper queen.

Why the hell did he have to be here, anyway?

"Given the specs of *Star of Kilri*, I think we have two Security Barcs docked," the woman said. "Plus one on close patrol like a beat cop hassling drunks."

Mafê Zariņš, that was her name, where Mafê was short for *Maria Fernanda*. Quiet, almost mousy. Shy around him, for reasons Oluchi had never bothered digging into. Not that it mattered. He had Anya and wouldn't trade her for anything.

Looking around, Oluchi was struck by something that really hadn't hit him until now, in spite of all the time he had spent aboard this ship. He was the only male on the bridge. Maybe the only one on the whole, immense ship.

It wasn't that Eduardo surrounded himself with beautiful women, although there was a surplus with this crew. Oluchi had spent too much time around Rio ships, where men outnumbered women something like five or six to one. But that was a cultural thing. A male chauvinism.

Yisan didn't have it.

Briefly, Oluchi wondered how many of these women might have originally been born in Rio Space, but chose to go someplace where their gender didn't work against them.

Antonia was looking at him as he realized he'd been wool-gathering.

"Huh?" he repeated helpfully.

"Do we take them?" she repeated. "According to everything Lazarus and the others have told me, *Celestial Sovereign* is in a different league, compared to Innruld Security Barcs, but we've never tried."

Oluchi considered his options. He wasn't anywhere in the chain of command, but he'd also more or less connived Antonia into almost everything she had done, when she might have just returned to Yisan. Oluchi wasn't sure where Eduardo was these days. Possibly on Brasilia negotiating the treaty that would upend all of the Human side of the galaxy by allying with Rio formally.

"If I told you I wanted an assassination instead of a mugging, would that clarify how I wanted you to do it?" he asked the Captain.

Antonia smiled. Nodded, even.

"Pilot, prepare to drop us into the position I have designated number seven," she turned and began issuing orders to her crew. "All guns are now unlocked. Everyone confirm your status."

Oluchi took a deep breath and tried to imagine what he'd just done. Anya leaned close enough to whisper in his ear.

"Just like in the vids," she said, kissing him while she was at it.

He turned to study her eyes.

"Lazarus makes it look easy," he offered in a shaky tone.

She nodded.

"Lots of practice killing people," she reminded him.

Yes, that was it. Lazarus was a killer. Addison as well. Hell, even Rod da Silva, back at Oton Mari.

Oluchi was much more like the Species Underground.

That epiphany nearly jarred his silly ass right out of the seat.

"What?" Anya asked, concern showing.

"Why they sent me," he whispered.

Around them, *Celestial Sovereign* was going through the final paces before a combat jump, a fox still at the edge of the clearing, spying on the sleeping chickens.

"Why what?" she asked, confused.

Oluchi tried to sort out the words before he spoke them, then gave up.

"All the other big players are killers," he unraveled for them. "Lazarus, Addison, da Silva. Even Eha, in her way."

Anya nodded patiently.

BLAZE WARD

"They sent me here because I'm not, at least by default," Oluchi continued. "I'll think about all the other things and come at it sideways, when Lazarus would just jump in there and immediately start stomping on everything that moves."

"We're doing that," she noted.

He nodded.

"But we still snuck in and just listened for a while, waiting for the blue-shift flash to reach them," Oluchi said. "I interface with the Species Underground better than anyone else because violence is not my first instinct."

"That's why I put up with your other foibles," she teased, kissing his cheek now.

"Madam, you're the exhibitionist, I shall remind you," he teased back, feeling everything fall into place now.

He'd been a gigolo. Worked his way up to Fixer, at least in his own mind, on the way to trying to turn the two of them into power players wealthy and important enough to sit at a table with Eduardo and negotiate deals.

But he could bridge this gap. The big one, divided down the middle by the Phraettis Nebula.

Oluchi Pryce could turn himself into the Ambassador that connected all sides, like some grand statesman.

Shit, this was going to be so much fun.

Just as soon as Antonia was done.

SIXTEEN

ANTONIA

CELESTIAL SOVEREIGN CAME through jump with a hard blue-shift, even over the short distance they'd moved. Antonia smiled. Esperança had dropped them exactly where she wanted, on the perfect heading.

"Adamanteia, open fire on target one," Antonia ordered simply. "Mafê, track those other two. I don't think we can get them if they stay close to the station, so we'll need to entice them out."

Both women answered and Antonia studied her screen.

Celestial Sovereign had been built as a heavily-protected escort by a man who hired professional pirates, and expected his business competition to do the same. Eduardo had even had a few pirates suggest improvements here and there, until this ship was nearly a Rio Protector escort for shielding and firepower.

So while she might be using it in ways Eduardo never expected, it was still nothing they weren't equipped to do.

"Firing now," Adamanteia called out as the two turrets on the sides opened up.

Celestial Sovereign was built as an oval, more or less, flat across the decks, wide, but extremely long. Two turrets retracted into the hull most of the time, so other pirates might not appreciate what they were facing. How many civilian ships this size mounted twinned Star Spears in turrets, with a Star Lance down the centerline?

Adamanteia held off on the Star Lance for now, as ordered. They might need to take a few potshots at ships in dock later, and Antonia didn't want those folks knowing how far she could reach if she came to rest and aimed.

And the first Security Barc was already coming apart at the seams, just from Adamanteia's first volley.

"Esperança, accelerate us up and away now," Antonia ordered. "Adamanteia, one more volley but try not to completely obliterate them."

She glanced over at Pryce and Persaud, noting that they were deep in some emotional conversation that didn't seem like a lover's spat, nor a strategy session she needed to worry about. And it kept him from asking stupid questions or giving her the sorts of orders she might just ignore.

Instead, the ship and her crew shifted around a long arc now. That Barc might be reduced to the scrap value of the hull, judging by the scans Mafê was echoing. At least they knew where the two lifepods were.

As Antonia watched, both blasted clear, up and down respectively, so the crew over there had made their own conclusions about where they stood.

"Esperança, get us to position eleven next," Antonia ordered. "Adamanteia, hold fire and track against anybody coming out of trans-space blind. Not expecting any help, but now would be when they sprang their own trap."

Antonia had held extensive conversations with Lazarus and Addison before they left, just so she could better understand the Innruld, if she was likely to end up doing exactly what she'd let Pryce and da Silva talk her into doing. She had an appreciation of the locals as being under-gunned Westphalian pricks in their own way.

"Emergency distress beacons in the air," Mafê called in a bored voice.

"Announce to the locals that anyone moving to rescue those pods is safe from us," Antonia ordered. "Tell them we're only here to kill Innruld Security Barcs, not to rob anyone."

A round of chuckles from her women warmed her. Antonia could imagine an entire crew of *men* growling or something equally macho and irrelevant right now. Governor Sonels had impressed upon Antonia that the Innruld divided the bottom rung of society from the top two, the Innruld themselves and their jackbooted thugs. Damaging those punks in the middle would do the most to knock the Innruld off their pedestal.

"I have two vessels launched from the station by blueshift," Mafê called sharply. "One of the Barcs just cleared locks. The other looks like a local freighter even weirder than Addison's."

"They calling our bluff on rescue?" Antonia replied.

She could move to three other positions from this one, if the two Barcs were using this as a position to try to crossfire her. But the locals needed to see her letting innocents be rescued.

That word would spread faster than any Innruld propaganda.

"Stand by," Mafê replied.

"Esperança, shift us to position eight anyway," Antonia decided. "Adamanteia, if that Barc starts our way, punish him, but ignore the freighter until they provoke you."

Calm. Heads down. Professional.

The locals were hideously outmatched here, and Antonia preferred it that way.

Eduardo might still fire her when this was all done.

But it would have been worth it.

SEVENTEEN

OLUCHI

OLUCHI HAD WATCHED PATIENTLY as that second Barc charged right into battle with *Celestial Sovereign*, only to have its bow kicked in by combined fire. Two freighters were chasing after escape pods now, once the first ship had been ignored.

That left the last Security Barc, still snugged up against the platform, and Bajerlie station itself.

This place followed the models Oluchi had learned about from Addison. A Skycity version, rather than the organic mess that was Oton Mari. An enormous castle that looked like it had been lifted into space and orbited, except that it had been built there. Four gates at the bottom, where small ships flew inside and got placed into one of forty-four bays. The slender, elegant towers rising above, representing money and power, well above the lower decks where *everyone else* lived.

Antonia turned to him with an expectant look. They had gone just about as far as their original planning could take them, if that last ship didn't want to die today. Not that he could blame them. That second Barc had fared even worse than the first, only launching one escape pod.

But then, the front third of the ship looked like someone had hit it with a small planet, as it tumbled away.

Anya was also studying his profile now.

Oluchi swallowed past a tongue that was a little thick.

"You haven't used the Star Lance yet, right?" he asked, uncertain whether or not he'd missed it.

"Correct," Antonia replied. "We have not."

"Based on Oton Mari and other things, do you think you could hurt the station from a safe distance?" Oluchi asked. "One where their guns were too weak to get through your shields?"

"Probably," she nodded. "Why?"

As is *Why bother?* Or *Are you that stupid?*

Oluchi smiled and suddenly found his footing, after several moments of *mushiness*.

"We're in the revolution business, Antonia," he reminded her. "Liberation. All that jazz. What happens if you start taking potshots at the station and he can't really fire back effectively?"

"That last Barc probably comes out and commits suicide?" she replied.

"Does he?" Oluchi pressed. "Or does he run like hell, bringing word of redcoats riding? Does he go to the nearest other system and try to get help, confident that he probably survives, because they would have to send back a big fleet to chase us off?"

"What's your game, Pryce?" Antonia asked. Not for the first time.

It was a common refrain from many of the women he'd known in a previous life. One he had even answered honestly, at least most of the time.

Today, Oluchi unhooked his safety harness and rose, making his way over to Maria Fernanda.

"Mafê, can you bring up a scan of the station itself?" he asked.

That woman glanced at her Captain and got permission first, but she did it.

"Skycity," he explained to the other women around him as he tapped the tower on the screen. "If you are rich and important, you live up there, rather than down in the tenements of the cargo level. That is just about all of Innruld Society graven in steel, ladies. I propose to snipe at this spot right here, and see if the Star Lance has the power to actually get through the shields at that one location."

"What does it gain you, to blow up that tower?" Adamanteia asked now.

"I'm willing to bet that the governor lives somewhere really close to that spot," Oluchi smiled. "He might be somewhere lower, like down in a station control room by now, but from what I've learned, the Innruld expect their peons to *just handle things*, so they might not have even told him that there were terrible, *Human* pirates outside. What happens if you blow up his house? Better, what happens to the station if he's home when you do it?"

Oluchi could not believe that he was actually counseling assassination, but there they were. Lazarus had said more than once that he just wanted to knock those slavers off their perch. Addison was the one who wanted to hunt them all down and exterminate the entire species.

A station like Bajerlie might not even have more than a few dozen Innruld aboard, as far as they were from anywhere interesting. Just their thugs in pretty suits. But what would the undercity do if all the overlords were suddenly dead?

He waited, aware that he was moving beyond a simple

pirate and into a fully-fledged revolutionary now. But he couldn't help it.

The Species Underground wanted to be free. And were counting on Humans like Oluchi Pryce to contribute.

He couldn't do it all, but he could show a few people the way.

And if others took it upon themselves to start assassinating Innruld toffs…

"If Eduardo fires me for this, you will find me a better gig," Antonia announced.

"Madam, you could probably become an admiral in the Species Underground Navy tomorrow if you chose to," Oluchi nodded. "But I promise I will protect you from Eduardo, at least as much as I can."

"Good enough," the captain nodded. "Adamanteia, you and Esperança line us up for a few shots. Mafê, keep watch on that last pigeon and see what he does when he detaches from the station."

Oluchi moved back to his chair and leaned against Anya's shoulder now. He'd have never gotten this far without her. Hopefully, she appreciated that.

They still had a future together that they had to discover.

And maybe shape.

EIGHTEEN

ANTONIA

SHE WOULD HAVE to give the man credit, but Antonia wasn't sure she'd say it too loud. He was already a bigshot, and she'd liked him more when there was still some humility to Oluchi Pryce.

But he'd been right.

The shielding on Bajerlie Station wasn't any better than on their ships. Worse, maybe, although she'd have to look at Mafê's readouts to be sure. At this range, a Star Lance wouldn't have been much more than a flashlight against most Human stations.

Here, it had been a blowtorch. Steel was steel, but there were limits to the thermal conductivity of the hull before it failed explosively. And it had.

The biggest tower was a third shorter now. A javelin of metal and a cloud of shards tumbled away, but they didn't have escape velocity, so they would eventually fall back into the atmosphere below.

"Is that last Barc fleeing?" Antonia asked Mafê.

"Negative, Captain," the woman replied. "Stuck close up

against the side. Do you suppose the crew abandoned ship while it was still attached to the station?"

"Not a bet I'll take," Antonia muttered, mostly under her breath.

She turned to Oluchi and Anya now. Watched the man silently draw strength from his usually-quiet partner in crime. As a man should.

"Open a hail to the station," he said in a quiet voice.

She'd known the man played a lot of poker with Eduardo. This sounded like that last call when you'd just drawn a fourth Queen.

Except that Oluchi had five queens in the room with him right now, so that might not be too far off.

"Channel open," Mafê replied.

"Bajerlie Station, this is the Species Underground warship *Celestial Sovereign*," he announced in a slow, methodical tone. "You will surrender to me, or I will destroy you right now."

Antonia wasn't sure who gasped, but it sounded like more than one of her women. But then, they hadn't understood where Pryce's mission was likely to take him. Antonia had seen it three days ago.

After all, everyone talked about how primitive Innruld technology was compared to the Humans. But none of them had really gone beyond those punk Security Barcs desperately in over their heads against a pocket escort like this to understand just how outclassed the Innruld were. And it wasn't fair even then. Hell, most pirates back home would have gotten their fur a little singed before they managed to flee from the surprises Antonia had tucked in on this yacht.

"*Celestial Sovereign*, this is Bajerlie Station Control," a tentative voice called back. "We refuse your demands."

"Fine," Oluchi said, his voice dropping a third in just one

syllable. "Gunner, kill another tower at the same height as the first one."

Antonia suppressed her own gasp now. The line was open, so whoever Pryce was talking to would also hear that command.

Adamanteia turned to her with eyes maybe a little bigger than normal, but this wasn't a battle anymore. This was a chicken against a farmer with an ax.

However, as Lazarus and others had said, there would be a lot of deaths before the Innruld finally understood that their time was over.

Antonia nodded to Adamanteia and held up three fingers, indicating the tower to target.

Adamanteia nodded and went back to her targeting. She and Esperança murmured quietly for a few moments, and then the ship rolled on gyros a little. Not much. Just enough to shift the bow, even though the Star Lance up there could have made the shot.

Those extra seconds would have to be terrifying, down at the receiving end.

A bolt lanced out and shattered the next tower into a bloody stump, steel and air exploding outwards in a cloud of plasma.

"Bajerlie Station Control, this will be the last time I ask," Oluchi announced. "You will surrender right now, or I will cut all communications and carve your station into fragments that will deorbit, while killing every single ship that comes within range of my guns while I do so. ***Do you understand me?***"

That long stretch of silence while the mind attempts to process something so terrible, so insane, that it is beyond reason. That the Lords of the Galaxy aren't even *relevant* today, let alone in charge.

Antonia found herself holding her breath, wondering if

those idiots over there would be willing to commit suicide and take everyone with them. She'd known a few fanatics in her day. Bad for business, whatever your business was.

All it would take would be one jackass deciding to call Oluchi's bluff.

Because Pryce wasn't bluffing right now. Antonia could see that in his eyes, facing past her to the screen showing the badly battered Skycity that was Bajerlie.

"*Celestial Sovereign*, this is Manager Draigheel," a new voice replied. "Director Narglash is no longer in command of this station. We surrender. Please do not destroy us."

Antonia watched Oluchi slump a little as he let go that terrible breath, poised on the verge of uttering the command for devastation, and returned a little closer to the playboy card sharp Antonia had once known. Oluchi was even sexier as a killer, but she didn't need all that playing out on her deck, and he had Anya. They were a matched pair that didn't look like they needed a third or a fourth to keep things interesting.

"Bajerlie, this is Ambassador Pryce, speaking for the Species Underground," Oluchi continued, maybe three shades less violent than he had been before. "You will put all the Innruld left on that last Security Barc, along with any loyalists who would rather flee than face justice for what they have done. Whoever commands that vessel will contact me before they separate from the station, so I don't just annihilate them on reflex, but if they are fleeing, I will let them go. Once all the so-called masters have fled with their tails between their legs, I will have further instructions."

He walked over to Mafê and tapped her on the shoulder, nearly making the poor woman leap out of her chair in surprise before she caught her breath.

Rather than speak, he leaned across and killed the comm

line himself, standing up and drawing a heavy breath before turning back to the rest of the room.

"Three deuces," he announced with an air of relief. "Not a weak hand, but not always a winning one. Thank you everyone for backing my bluff."

"You weren't bluffing, Pryce," Antonia smiled. She gestured at the rest of the room. "Five Queens. Always a winner."

NINETEEN

EHA

EHA WATCHED Addison playing peekaboo with Adriana. The little one had only ever known one other Churquen, Alla, so having a third one was endlessly fascinating. And it let her bond with her father, in a way that Eha hoped would lead to a close lifetime relationship unlike her own experience.

Her father, Nixus Dunham, was a vague memory, as he'd disappeared in a random Innruld sweep when Eha was ten. And then never emerged again from prison, having caught some disease that killed him when the masters didn't bother with medicine for prisoners.

Alla had already been something of a revolutionary. That loss had turned her into a killer. One who had raised her own daughter into the family business.

Eha wanted Adriana to know her father. If not for this ongoing war, she would have suggested that he quit the Rio Navy and join her on Liberty or Brasilia. But she knew that they were nowhere close to that day.

So she coiled on the bed of their shared cabin and watched him on the floor with a giggling kit.

Addison's head came up and locked eyes with her. She watched him scoop Adriana up and coil her around his arm as he slithered closer.

Never spoke, just leaned in and kissed her. But it was what she had needed, and he'd seen it before she had.

Something melted off her back scales and her keel was suddenly lighter. She leaned back and the three of them ended up coiled and twined on the bed, snuggling.

"What aren't you telling me?" Addison whispered, still nuzzling her ear as Adriana giggled with joy.

Eha tried not to tense, but he felt it.

She sighed and kissed him.

"Erlyn thinks that Westphalia will redouble their efforts to assassinate me," she replied quietly, letting a squirming ball of silliness crawl between them, searching for a warm spot. "That was part of the reason we're going back to the colony, where things are more carefully controlled."

"Except that we've taken on another crew of sailors at Brasilia," Addison noted. "They are all strangers to Lazarus and the others."

She felt herself nod, but there were really no words. Lucas would protect her as best he could, but he was the only person she really knew well.

"It will be better when we arrive," she assured him now. "Admiral Santos is sending *Ajax* and *Recife* forward, so I will make a point to remain with my mother and the other colonists, along with Erlyn, Pascia, and their bodyguards."

"Will you be safe?" he asked.

"None of us are ever safe, Addison Wolcott," she retorted. "You and I have been in this business for a long enough time to appreciate that."

"Yes, but until recently, I didn't have a reason to worry," he said. "Now, I have two. And you are far more important than I am."

He hugged her tighter, coiled protectively. Eha enjoyed it, but he was right. They would go off to battle again, and she would need to remain on Liberty, where she could possibly trust none of the Humans she encountered.

How did she turn the Churquen and Yithadreph refugees she knew from revolutionaries into killers?

TWENTY

LAZARUS

LAZARUS SAT at his desk and listened to the two High Councilors finish their explanation.

"Does Carlos know?" he asked, boiling it all down.

"Admiral Santos sent orders and messages for him and his command staff only," Teixeira replied. "I wanted you specifically to know what we suspect. Intelligence agencies are working, but you of all people will understand how complicated that can be."

"Councilor Teixeira, you aren't supposed to know those things about me," Lazarus replied evenly.

"When you became this important to the Rio Alliance, I demanded a full briefing, Lazarus," she said. "As Chair of the Council Security Committee, I have the highest security clearance allowed. So, yes, I am supposed to know those things. I am aware that you used to be an assassin for the Navy, Captain. And all the other things you've done since then that ended up with you sitting in that chair today to talk to us. About the only things I don't know about you are the things nobody is willing to talk about from your time with Addison and Aileen, but I expect those stories to come out eventually."

Lazarus grimaced and compressed his lips. Erlyn Teixeira was on his side, as much as any Human could be. She had already bent over backwards to help them in Innruld Space, but he had a hard time letting himself trust anyone. Grace had almost been too much.

He already knew that there were spies in the government. One of them had nearly gotten him killed. That would have been rude, but anyone going after Eha would have to climb over his dead body to get there.

It would be Yisan all over again if they did, except it would be him firing the Kirov instead of Addison.

He relented and drew a breath to speak about the time that the other Councilor, Nkali, was going to chime in.

"I designed the ambassadorial quarters well aft," Lazarus reminded them. "That's actually a module that can be pulled out and replaced with something else, but we never built another one before all this happened. Eha would be safe back there, but she doesn't have a full staff of people. Hell, she doesn't even have a cook, since Khyaa'sha runs the forward kitchen where me, Kuei, and Wybert eat. If she's at risk from some crew member of mine, she'd either have to remain trapped aft, or stay on Liberty. What's safer? Or do we just assign Lucas to her permanently?"

He got to watch those two women stew now. Lazarus had never had a particularly high opinion of politicians, but these two were working to make the galaxy better, rather than just aggregating power and privilege unto themselves, like so many he'd known in his time.

"If we start jumping at ghosts, Westphalia wins," Councilor Nkali announced. "I will not have it. Captain, when we get to Liberty, I will have a conversation with Alla Dunham about adding a full staff of Churquen and

Yithadreph assistants and minders to Eha's Embassy. I need her forward with you, so she can talk to everyone with firsthand knowledge. Plus, Addison and your older crew members will move heaven and earth to protect her in ways that Rio marines might not. I cannot think of any place in this galaxy that she would be safer than aboard *Ajax*, where at least the risks can be contained. If I thought I could order it, Xiuying Bălan would be transferred and promoted, and bring some of his people with him."

"You don't need him," Lazarus interrupted her.

"Why not?" Nkali asked.

"Because we already have someone who would make an exceptional bodyguard for Eha," he smiled.

"Better than Commander Bălan?"

"Xiuying is nervous around her," Lazarus said.

Erlyn Teixeira's eyes lit up with sudden realization. Nkali felt it, because she turned to her fellow Councilor and looked at the woman pointedly.

"Will she?" Teixeira asked.

"She would, for me," Lazarus said. "But you might make it official by asking yourself."

"Consider that done," Teixeira nodded, and then turned to her compatriot.

"He's right," she said. "Everyone always overlooks the woman because she works so hard to remain quiet and unassuming. But that's by training, isn't it?"

That last sent in his direction, so Lazarus nodded.

"Who are you talking about?" Nkali finally demanded. "Who do you have that is so dangerous that you're both confident that this person can protect Ambassador Dunham?"

"Grace Savidge, Pascia," Teixeira said.

"The woman from Yisan?" Nkali asked, still confused. "What does she do?"

"She was trained as a geisha, Councilor Nkali," Lazarus said.

"And?"

"And she's the most dangerous being I have ever met in my life, and you two know what I used to do for a living."

TWENTY-ONE

ANYA

ANYA HAD SPENT TOO many years as a spy. She found it hard to step outside of that role as a quiet, almost mousy bureaucrat, deep in the bowels of the system. Even her more amorous adventures with Oluchi had been geared towards drawing the man in. Although he was right about how the risk of being caught had been a thrill.

In her old job, she could never do anything interesting, lest someone start paying closer attention to the real woman and blow her cover.

Whoever the real Anya Persaud had been. The old one.

The new one was standing next to a gambler and ex-gigolo, with her own pistol in a holster where she could get at it quickly as the airlock began to cycle.

Anya knew that Oluchi was a killer. And not just a ladykiller. If she was going to keep standing next to him in public, she needed to reach into a new role today and find that person.

It helped that Captain Veracruz—Antonia—had a couple of women standing close by with larger weapons in hand.

Those two looked like killers, but Eduardo Martìnez had probably hired them for exactly that job.

Anya Persaud looked at the pair of them and then split the difference back to Oluchi.

Yes. There.

She kicked a hip out with a bit of a flare that lowered one shoulder and kinked her spine. It brought her shooting hand to rest on the handle of the pistol and hitched her shoulders in an interesting invitation.

In a bar, it would be for someone to walk up and ask her to dance, if they had the courage. She supposed it was the same question here, just with a different meaning to *dance*.

She could do this.

"All hands," Oluchi announced as the airlock started to move. "Company imminent."

Antonia was monitoring audio. Plus she had a couple of other women hidden nearby, in case the Humans needed to clear these decks with beam fire from an attempted ambush by the locals.

The woman in the airlock was Churquen. Another was visible, deeper back in the shuttle that had carried a purported representative of the Species Underground out to *Celestial Sovereign* to negotiate.

Lighter scales than Eha or Alla, almost up to the color of fine jade, with stripes running her length that flashed somewhere between bronze and black, depending on the light.

She was unarmed, as instructed.

Oluchi bowed to the woman.

"Madam Tersand, I am Oluchi Pryce, Ambassador to many places, but currently representing the Species Underground forces holding Oton Mari," the man said.

Anya realized with a start that he was the only male in the room, including the other crewmembers on the shuttle.

She was from the Rio Alliance. Male chauvinism was so baked in that she occasionally forgot that Yisan and Innruld Space weren't anywhere near as male dominated.

"Ambassador Pryce," the stranger bowed back. "You are all Human?"

"This is a Human vessel, Ambassador Tersand," Oluchi said with a smile, followed by a grand sweep of one arm that thankfully didn't hit anyone. "Please, let us retire to the lounge and relax. We have tea and juice that will be safe for a Churquen. I am the assistant to two such women, and have had extensive dealings with both Churquen and Yithadreph, as well as a dozen or so others."

He led. She ended up next to the Churquen woman as something of an escort as the others followed, but Anya had spent enough time around Eha that she knew the pace and movement.

Eduardo's lounge had been assembled by a man with more money than places to spend it, so he'd made everything elegantly comfortable. Deep carpet under her feet. Walls a soft brown somewhere darker than bleached sand but not stark. Woodwork handcrafted by experts as decoration on cabinets.

Even adapting things more recently for the comfort of other species hadn't taken that much glamour off it, other than to remove about half of the breakfast nook and replace that bench with the kind of seats that could be adjusted for Aileen, Thadrakho, Khyaa'sha, or Eha.

Anya served tea. She would have preferred coffee, but few of the species liked the bitterness. And most detested the jitteriness of the caffeine.

Niela Tersand watched them all like a king cobra bothered from a nap. But she sipped at her tea, once everyone else had gotten mugs from the same pot and enjoyed them.

Anya set a second pot to brewing as they studied each other.

"Your masters, such as they call themselves, have departed?" Oluchi asked.

"The survivors have," Tersand replied with a ghost of a smile, there in the eyes. "It took four freighters, packed to the tips, to haul off everyone who wanted to display their loyalty to the Innruld. Now what?"

"Now, you send a messenger to Oton Mari," Oluchi replied. "We will get there before they do, unless we carry them ourselves, but you'll want to send a ship anyway, so they can get back later. Chera Sonels is the new governor at Oton Mari. She's Tarni."

"There have been rumors of a new species, attacking and destroying everything in their path," Tersand noted without asking a question.

"That would be Humans," Anya decided to speak up, lest the stranger think Oluchi the only one not mute here. "Us. But we are here to liberate the Species Underground from the Innruld."

"And the devastation you have caused?" Tersand looked around.

It was really just the three of them, but Antonia had several women standing around as guards, as well as protecting the airlock.

"A Human warship has been hunting Innruld Security Pyramids," Oluchi smiled. "They have captured three of them at Oton Mari and upgraded them to better technology. You'll want to do the same here at Bajerlie."

"Hunting?" Tersand asked, her jaw falling open and the scales around her eyes flaring as far out as they would go.

"That's correct," Anya also smiled. "Lazarus has killed more than ten others so far, before they started to flee as soon as his ship appeared."

A bit of a tall tale, if only because those stupid Pyramids took twenty minutes to power up their trans-space drives. Far more than *Ajax* needed to harpoon them if he timed his jumps.

"And you are not here to conquer?" Tersand asked.

"We're here to kill Innruld," Oluchi replied in a voice so disinterested that Anya did a double-take. "And their lackeys, whoever decides to remain loyal to that cause. The rest are to be freed, and then we'd like to start trading with you."

"If you are that advanced, what could Innruld Space possibly produce that your kind would find interesting?" the Churquen woman demanded.

Anya liked the way Oluchi's eyes twinkled.

"What have you got to sell?"

TWENTY-TWO

LAZARUS

THE CIVILIANS HAD all departed *Ajax* to go to the surface of the Liberty colony. That was proper, as things would be entirely military from here, and Lazarus could sleep by himself for a few days while Grace was down protecting Eha from any threats that might arise.

They were in the main conference room today. Him, Addison, Carlos Nguema, Paulo Quispe. Marie Oslor had joined them, but she was handling communications for the flotilla. Still, she had apparently impressed the hell out of Addison, back on *Dutra*.

"So I have read everything that Admiral Santos has sent along with you, Lazarus," Carlos began. "I suppose that I should be thrilled to be put in command of a raid such as this, but I also got the impression from his notes that I should continue listening to you, unlike some of the starchier admirals out there. Thoughts?"

"We've defended Vilga's Stand three times now," Lazarus said. "Twice in the last two years. It has become a symbol of just about everything right with the Rio Alliance and wrong with Westphalia. I think he's wanting the symbolism of us launching at attack back from here."

"And *Ajax*?" Quispe asked.

But then, he'd never seen the Kirov Lance used in battle.

"*Ajax* exists to hurt Heavy Starcruisers, Captain," Lazarus smiled. "*Gotland* learned that the hard way. I know that Santos was all set on letting you just show up and see what the odds were when we got there, but *Ajax* radically changes those calculations for everyone."

"And your latest new crew?" Quispe asked, with a grin on his face.

"The folks I pulled off of *Recife* for that first battle will always have a berth with me, Paulo," Lazarus grinned back. "If I thought I could get any off the station ahead of you, I would. Right now, I'm running short, but nowhere near the skeleton crew I had before."

"Are we better off swapping out some of the crews?" Carlos asked. "I understand that *Recife* replaced everyone they sent on, but I'm in charge here, at least until the Bureau of Personnel catches up with us."

Lazarus considered speaking up, but held his tongue. Everyone had heard his theories of Westphalian spies and didn't need those to be repeated. He had no way of telling if any of his new sailors were double agents, and it would be an insult to honest sailors to put them ashore on a station, just before sailing off to battle.

He would rely on Grace to protect Eha. There literally was nobody better trained for that task, and Lazarus had been in the business for twenty years at this point.

He pivoted to a different topic now.

"What resources will you be taking, Admiral?" he asked Carlos, putting everything to one side.

"Santos left that up to me, balancing defense of Liberty and two High Councilors against forward force. He did sent

Curitiba and her whole squadron to replace *Recife*, so I can take all my Light Starcruisers, plus *Ajax*. That leaves two Heavy Starcruisers and a bunch of escorts here, but I plan to get a little sneaky."

"How so?" Addison asked, breaking out of his normal quiet when discussing military matters. "What risks are we introducing to the system?"

"Because the station is fully operational, I can put *PL-371* and her consorts, *P-4491* and *P-4502*, directly under your command as part of another raiding force," Carlos replied. "You will accompany us to Esmer and assist in that assault."

"And afterwards?" Lazarus asked carefully.

Carlos had used the phrase *another raiding force* as if *Ajax* might not remain in tandem with *Recife*. Not that Lazarus had *considered* committing insubordination yet again, or anything.

Carlos smiled, like he could read minds.

"We will determine our next course of action once we see what we can do to Esmer," he replied. "It might be that we split into two forces to hit secondary targets. Or one team might pull back to protect the vicinity of Liberty while the other does…*things*."

Things.

Carlos had been with him in the Phraettis Nebula. Had fought a ScoutWall and beaten them. As near as Lazarus could tell, his commanding admiral was more or less giving Lazarus permission to return to Innruld Space after this, and maybe even take a squadron of Protectors with him.

No Security Barc in Innruld Space would last ten minutes against those three ships dropping out of jump on top of it. And Carlos knew that.

"Questions?" Carlos asked in a leading way, but Lazarus shook his head. Addison did the same. "In that case, we are adjourned. Everyone let your forces know that I plan to make the first jump forward in roughly ninety hours from now, so plan your repair cycles accordingly. We'll move in three pieces. I'll send the Light Starcruiser *Paraná* and half of my escorts first, with *Recife* and *Ajax* to rendezvous later."

Everyone rose and started to depart, but Lazarus caught Carlos's eye and the man remained behind. Quickly, they were alone.

"What's up, Lazarus?" Carlos asked.

"I have a question, but you don't have to answer it," he said. Still, Carlos nodded. "Are you serious about letting *Ajax* roam free after Esmer? What did Santos say?"

"In fairly ambiguous terms, he let me know that you are a menace to the proper operation of a bureaucratic navy," Carlos laughed. "But that bureaucracy was likely to get in the way of doing what was right. He also reminded me that *technically*, you are still attached to the Bureau of Research, and not to the frontline fleet, so *technically* we can't give you orders, until such time as *Ajax* has been *properly* accepted into service."

"So all this is an extended shakedown cruise?" Lazarus asked with wonder.

"Proof of concept, as it were," Carlos said with a grin. "At some point, someone will demand you return to service and act like a sailor, but right now he expects you to continue acting like a pirate and revolutionary, though he never used those words."

"What about *PL-371* and her two?" Lazarus asked. "They are under orders."

"Technically," Carlos began, and then paused to chuckle. "However, I have attached them to your squadron now, so please don't do anything with them that gets me fired, okay?"

"Don't immediately sell them to the Species

Underground, you mean?" Lazarus asked, wondering what the limits might really be. "Is that what I'm hearing?"

"Not all three of them," Carlos replied, causing Lazarus to recoil a little. "In fact, it would probably be best in the long run if you just ended up recruiting about a third of a crew for each of them, so we had the nucleus of a trained navy over there. I could see Pedro Santos doing a technology transfer. Those escorts are a little old and long in the tooth these days, but we've had to keep every ship in service as long as possible to keep Westphalia off our necks. At the same time, those things would be hell on wheels in Innruld Space. You've crippled one Heavy Starcruiser and I've captured a second, so Westphalia has to be feeling the pinch. More so after we hit Esmer and then do whatever we do."

"Pity that nothing the Species Underground fields could join us in battle," Lazarus nodded. "That would really ram home the shape of the future."

"We'll burn that bridge when we get there, Lazarus," Carlos nodded as well. "For now, let's take *Ajax* and go hammer some people."

TWENTY-THREE

EDUARDO

EDUARDO LIKED to think of it as his legacy. He had started with practically nothing more than sixty years ago. Just gumption and brains, and turned that into one of the largest trading companies in space, Human or otherwise. While he didn't own Yisan outright, he had the most shares. And the greatest reach.

This morning, he was on his shady porch, enjoying the pleasant morning sun as it burned off the fog and revealed his vast back yard. Janice had delivered more coffee and then vanished back inside while he worked his way through the news and various reports.

He looked up when Collin appeared, a travel mug steaming in one hand and a briefcase in the other. Eduardo nodded him to the other chair and smiled. All of his children would inherit his fortune, one of these days, but Eduardo had added a couple of surprises, including a share of things for Collin.

The kids were all pretty good at business, and his grandchildren would never starve, but none of the next generation had the fire to make themselves rich had they started with nothing. But he didn't hold that against them. Their great-grandchildren wouldn't go hungry, unless someone royally screwed up.

But Eduardo saw a great deal of himself in Collin Lau. How he had been fifty or more years ago.

"Any surprises?" Eduardo asked as the man settled and began pulling folders.

Eduardo liked the feel of ink on paper. It added a solidity and solemnity you couldn't get on a screen.

"Of everyone, Fernanda Flores seems to be the only one who had figured out what we were up to," Collin began, handing him a folder. "The rest jumped in after she did, so old hulls are almost impossible to find, but we got most of the good ones and she probably got the rest. Every shipyard anyone owns is ramping up to run around the clock for the next three years, and I've already taken the liberty to rearrange capital to start two new ones for you."

"Two?" Eduardo asked, opening the folder to scan the executive summary.

"One dedicated to a new class of long-hauler," Collin replied, "Making runs from Yisan to places in Innruld Space, or Yisan to Brasilia. We'll be able to dominate bulk cargo on those sorts of runs. Margins will be slender, but better than anyone else will be able to achieve, plus we'll be at a greater scale."

"I see," Eduardo nodded. "And the other?"

"I've probably watched too many vids, Eduardo," Collin laughed. "On the screen, it always looks so romantic to be flying around in a tramp freighter, hauling small cargoes point to point and having adventures. They skip the parts where the ships break down constantly, gets attacked by pirates, and runs with a tremendous mortgage whose payments never fade."

Eduardo chuckled. He'd watched those same sorts of vids

as a young man, but he'd seen through the fairy tale quickly and gotten himself into the corporate meetings as soon as he could afford to buy his way in. From there, he'd leveraged himself all the way up to this chair, this manor, and this estate.

"So what are we doing to serve the tramp business?" he asked his *Assistant Business Manager*.

On a business card, Collin Lau's title wasn't all that impressive, until you realized that the Business Manager of Martìnez Holdings was Eduardo himself.

"Instead of building complicated things, we're using as much open source technology as we can," Collin replied. "That means fewer licensing fees. In addition, most of the ship is empty inside, with holes drilled in the deck of every cabin where furniture can be added or moved around. The bridge comes with the most bare bones flight station we could get away with and still meet safety regulations."

Eduardo smiled as the implications became clear.

"Every member of the Species Underground will have to customize the vessel to their own physiology anyway," he nodded with understanding. "I presume we'll be opening other factories to build those parts?"

"I'm out-sourcing that aspect for now," Collin said. "That way we can extend new licenses to folks in Innruld Space as we identify factories we want to do business with. Or build ourselves with local investors."

"Which Oluchi Pryce and Anya Persaud will be identifying for us," Eduardo smiled. "I like it."

"I figured we'd end up only making them for Churquen and Yithadreph if we tried to do it ourselves, so I'm also financing a design studio at the Liberty colony to take advantage of their expertise while we can," Collin said. "Then we'll sell those designs. In three years, a prospective captain ought to be able to order a basic hull, perhaps with a few upgrades during construction, but otherwise right off the lot, and then they can order all the components they need for their species right out of a catalog, either to be installed at the factory, or done by a middleman."

"Have we had a chance to work with their trans-space drives?" Eduardo asked. "Can they be upgraded or modernized to the point that they make sense to use instead of stardrives?"

"We have not," Collin shook his head ruefully. "Should we look to endow a Chair of Research at some university's technology incubator? That would crystallize research somewhere."

"Do it on Brasilia, or one of the big Rio worlds," Eduardo decided. "That keeps them engaged, but gives us the benefit of any breakthroughs. I don't expect any, but you never discount the impossible."

"Will do," Collin said.

Eduardo took a sip of his coffee and studied the young man.

"I have a personal question now, Collin," he began.

Collin got a little nervous, as he was normally a private individual. Still, he steeled himself and nodded.

"Have you heard from Marie Oslor?"

Collin flinched, but he should have known that his boss would be paying attention to those sorts of things.

Collin took a quick drink of his own coffee and blushed.

"I have," he mumbled.

"Was it good news?"

"It might be?" Collin hazarded a guess. "She's been promoted to serve the admiral in command of the Liberty system, which is now Carlos Nguema. They are aboard the Heavy Starcruiser *Recife* at this moment, which was Rod da Silva's command before that."

"So she is at the center of things," Eduardo noted. "And

probably thinking about her career rather than what might come after it. Or perhaps instead?"

He watched Collin deflate a little, but Eduardo understood. He'd had to chase hard after Deena in order to convince her and her family that he would amount to more than another hard-scrabble punk with a dream.

"Perhaps, young man, you should consider personally touring this new design studio you intend to come into being at Liberty," Eduardo observed, feeling wicked and maybe a little mean. But kids occasionally needed to be prodded out of the nest. "Make sure everything is exactly as I would want it, rather than relying on whatever agent you intended to send."

That sudden gleam of hope in Collin's eyes would make the rest of his week, Eduardo decided, regardless of what happened.

"I might be a while," Collin replied, forever tied to business, even when now was perhaps the time to chase after personal matters.

"I have apparently sent Oluchi Pryce deep into Innruld Space, according to his last update," Eduardo noted. "That means I need someone keeping track of happenings in Rio Space as well. I will leave it up to the two of you to figure out how to get messages back and forth."

"Should we invent a Galactic Post?" Collin asked, perhaps a bit flippantly, because he stopped short when Eduardo suddenly smiled.

"Yes, exactly that," he said. "Take four of those hulls you have purchased. The four with the best engines and good enough firepower to protect themselves. Put crews you trust aboard, and start sequencing them through Akeley's Passage to Oton Mari for now. We'll expand that to other places as Lazarus and Oluchi roll up the Innruld. While you are at it, we'll need forward operating bases and trade stations in the

Nebula and on the far side. Plus, Lazarus was smart enough to start a bank here on Yisan. We'll need to invest a significant portion of funds and issue bonds on it to open branches in Species Underground systems as we identify them. Get me a preliminary draft before you depart for Liberty, and I'll handle the rest."

"You, Eduardo?" Collin asked.

"I might have taught you everything you know about finance, Collin," Eduardo smiled. "But not everything I know. If we're going to conquer the galaxy, let's do it the right way."

TWENTY-FOUR

EHA

EHA HAD HARDLY RECOGNIZED the city as they flew overhead. Now that they'd landed, she wondered if she had gone to the wrong planet. The hospital stood exactly on the ridgeline of the hill. The government building was there across the way, tiny on a huge plot of land originally saved for more buildings, if they were needed. But that would be a park for a while.

Road and paths led down to the river on both sides of the peninsula. Eha shuddered, but the Yithadreph would love it. Churquen didn't swim. They sank exceptionally well, so they avoided water, but the Yithadreph would fill in the whole bank of the river and be in heaven.

But the amount of construction utterly astounded her.

Landed now, the shuttle ramp dropped, admitting the mid-afternoon breeze off the water. It carried flowers and other scents Eha didn't recognize.

"Welcome home," Grace said as she rose from her seat and made her way close.

Eha shook her head.

"No, this is just the place we're staying," she corrected the tall Human woman. "I think that for both of us, home is aboard *Ajax*."

Grace nodded and they moved to the ramp, watching several vehicles driving closer, now that the shuttle was safely down.

Eha was not armed, but Grace was, with a pistol on her hip and several other things tucked in carefully. Eha had always thought that Humans were dangerous and violent, but watching Grace move through her dances, she had underestimated them. Grace was probably the most lethal person Eha would ever meet.

Lazarus held that opinion as well.

The sound of the ramp had woke Adriana, who poked out of her basket now, all wide-eyed and happy.

"Gram?" she asked as Eha picked the basket up.

"Gram," Eha agreed. "Soon, little one."

The Humans had agreed that Churquen tended to mature a little faster than Humans did, so that at one year old, she was verbal and moving around, where a Human child would just barely be learning such things.

That just meant that Eha had to keep a closer watch on the little pixie, lest she slither off and find someone to charm for cookies. On Liberty colony not everyone would have already been warned not to ruin someone's dinner.

The day was warm as they emerged into the sun. Eha felt the heat baking her scales, so she flexed everything up for the breeze. She wondered how it would be to sweat like a Human did. Like Grace was in the process of doing.

But Churquen also liked higher temperatures than Humans, and most of the time Eha had been a little chilled. Yet another reason to pick out this location on this world. Warm enough for Churquen, wet enough for Yithadreph, centralized against what the Humans would do when they were eventually allowed to colonize outside the reservation.

Alla emerged from the nearer truck and Eha made her way over, Adriana riding like a queen in her chariot as they did.

"GRAM!"

Eha got a coiled hug. Grace's was a little more sedate, but Humans didn't have the sorts of balance as a Churquen.

Most of them, anyway. Grace was probably an exception there, as well.

Eha suffered being inspected.

"Where's that pirate of yours?" Alla demanded, even as Adriana was racing up one arm and coiling happily onto the older woman's shoulder.

"Above us in orbit," Eha replied. "He and Lazarus will be departing again shortly, and nobody knows how long they will be gone."

"So he's afraid to face me?" Alla smiled and then turned to Grace. "Are you staying?"

Grace smiled and looked at Eha.

"Actually, both of us are only on the ground for a few days," Eha replied. She gestured to the two women standing off to one side. "You remember Erlyn Teixeira. And this is Pascia Nkali, also on the High Council. They will be here longer before returning to Brasilia."

"Charmed," Alla nodded, moving the conversation over that way in her role as colonial governor. Erlyn got a hug. Pascia did as well, which surprised Eha. She hadn't thought the older woman to be that tactile.

Perhaps she was just that much a politician.

"Let us all retire to my palace," Alla laughed, gesturing them to the vehicles. "There we can talk."

TWENTY-FIVE

ERLYN

ERLYN HAD SPENT much time around Alla on the flight back from Gowook. Being governor suited the woman, just from the things Erlyn had seen as they moved from the spaceport to the government hall. Things were clean and well organized. Streets were laid out following the curve of the land, instead of being cut for maximum efficiency, but the Churquen didn't ever think in straight lines.

This building was done in a style almost reminiscent of Georgian, but there were only so many ways to make a government hall look impressive, and columns out front were a cheap way to manage it.

Coffee was available only because Erlyn had known to pack a few pounds of beans with her and a small altar to reduce them to loveliness, while everyone else had worked through all the forms of tea that the Species Underground had brought with them and planted in pots, hoping to be able to grow them in Human-infected soil.

But Erlyn had always planned ahead.

Alla would be a worthwhile opponent if it ever came to that, but such wasn't the mission. Not even Pascia was going to be a problem, because by being here, that freed Carlos and Lazarus up to go shatter Westphalian shipping and ships.

This was a civilian room. Grace stood quietly off in one corner, but had already made it clear that she did not intend to talk today. She was guarding Eha and nothing more. All the sailors were in orbit, except for some marines landed to do engineering work, most of it outside the reservation boundaries, so that there was space prepared to expand the starport later, as well as flood control and such.

Humans were not scheduled to even be allowed on the surface otherwise for fourteen more years, and it would take a vote of the High Council to override that. Lucky that there were two High Councilors present.

"To what do I owe the honor of such esteemed guests?" Alla asked when everyone was finally settled with mugs of tea or coffee.

Erlyn looked around, but there were only three important people in this lounge: her, Pascia, and Eha. Plus Adriana.

"It is a bit of a shell game," Erlyn explained.

"Oh?"

Erlyn noted Eha's subtle nod to her mother.

"By sending a delegation to Liberty, we wanted to show the rest of the galaxy how much we valued our latest friends and colonists," Erlyn explained. "At the same time, the Fleet wanted to launch an attack on a Westphalian world, and decided to do it from here. There are nearly three squadrons of warships overhead, and about half will be departing in a few days."

"I see," Alla turned to her daughter. "And you're departing with them, you and Grace."

"Yes, ma'am," Eha replied, sounding like a teenager who had just been caught sneaking out after curfew.

Not that Erlyn had *any* experience with something like *that*.

"And Adriana?" Alla asked.

Eha gasped in surprise. So did Erlyn.

"Leave her here?" Eha asked.

"She'll be around her own kind," Alla reminded her. "Plus, there will be more births soon, so she'll have folks to grow up around. Just as your pirate Addison never knows when to call it good enough, I suspect that my hard-headed daughter might be the same way."

Erlyn grinned, struggling to suppress the giggles. That described both of them.

Then Alla turned her attention this way, and Erlyn sobered quickly. Like getting caught after curfew again.

"How long will you stay?" she asked, about as loaded a question as Erlyn could have imagined.

"We'd like to spend a goodly amount of time here," Erlyn replied. "I know many of you from Gowook, but Pascia has previously been…perhaps on the other side of some disagreements with me. She wants to learn about the Species Underground and the people who will be joining the Rio Alliance."

"The other side?" Alla asked, turning to Pascia.

Seriously, that woman had her *Mom-look* down solid, to watch the older Pascia blush and stammer under that social assault.

"The High Council used—*USED*—to be dominated by two groupings," Erlyn leaped in to rescue her cohort. "They might have been called the Alliance Block and the Humanist Block. But those sorts of things are melting now under the current pressures. Pascia is an ally, and we're trying to figure out the best way to win the war so that the Species don't necessarily have to flee their homes and lives in order to start over on a colony somewhere. Some might, and would be welcome, but we'd rather it not be *necessary*."

Pascia nodded too quickly. *Mom-look*, and all that.

"Well, the solution to that is rather obvious, isn't it?" Alla asked.

It wasn't. At least not to Erlyn. Nor Eha, from the confused way her scales flexed. Pascia looked lost. Adriana was the only one having fun here, not counting her grandmother.

"Send help to Oluchi Pryce," Alla said. "You can blow up Westphalia just like you will Innruld, but you need trade. To do that, he'll need ships. Fortunately, Eduardo Martìnez has already started planning and executing ahead of you."

Erlyn felt her stomach lurch. The Merchant Princes of Yisan had already invaded Innruld Space? Or were about to?

"Oh, it's not that bad," Alla laughed and grinned at them.

"What's he done?" Eha asked with perhaps a little more exasperation than Alla's laugh warranted.

"He's buying ships," Alla said. "Small ones that he will sell to our folks back on the other side. But he and Fernanda are also sending Human engineers here to work with us to design goods for the Species, so at the same time he is buying a lot of goodwill."

"Oh?" Erlyn asked.

She'd met Fernanda, back when there was some question about which of them Oluchi might try to seduce. Anya was always going to win that hands down, but Erlyn and Fernanda looked remarkably alike from any distance. The only serious difference was the amount of money Mistress Flores had in her bank account.

"They want to hire some of our colonists to consult. Designing consumer goods for Innruld Space," Alla smiled. "That's money coming into the colony, and goods that will sell better when you've won the war. But you'll need warships, and that costs money."

"And increased trade will generate more tax revenue," Pascia spoke, filling in the last hole. "You've given this much thought, Mistress Dunham."

"I need you to win the war, Councilor Nkali," Alla replied, *Mom-look* turning deadly serious now. "I cannot think of a better way to go about it than that. The Species cannot contribute much, but we must give all we can to this alliance, and do so right now."

TWENTY-SIX

CARLOS

CARLOS LOOKED OVER THE BRIDGE. Like Rod da Silva before him, Carlos believed in being at the center of the action, rather than down in the flag bridge. It was noisier, with two teams of folks talking, but he could filter out pieces and hear everything.

You never knew when something someone might have ignored would turn out to be critical.

"Marie, how are our four Lights doing?" he turned and asked Lt. Oslor.

There'd been a reason he'd brought her with him from *Dutra*. She could juggle all the information he needed in her head while updating it constantly. She didn't even look up from her screen right now.

"*Mendoza*, *Resistencia*, and *Paraná* are in forward escort positions," she replied. "Protectors are arrayed outside that. *Ajax* is on our upper right rear flank, pretending to be another escort."

He grunted. Thin, but maybe someone would be stupid enough to fall for it. If *Ajax* was truly an escort, it would be dead astern, either high or low, depending on the impending plane of battle. Anything to keep other Starcruisers or a GunWall off of *Recife*'s ass in the coming mess.

But he and Lazarus had discussed it, and there was always a chance that someone wasn't paying attention and just thought that there was a Light Starcruiser back there, rather than a wall of Agincourt archers.

The English hadn't been useful for much, but there'd been a stretch of about six or eight centuries where their culture had come to dominate most of Earth before later fading into oblivion. Carlos still found himself using Englishisms in his vernacular from time to time.

"Update," Marie snapped loud enough that Paulo looked up as well. "Scouts have just returned and are transmitting reports."

Carlos nodded and studied things as they came up.

He'd brought the force out more than a light-year from Esmer proper and waited while he sent some Protector/Scouts down into the sunlight to take the temperature. Nobody had pulled a raid on Westphalia with this many cruisers in years. Maybe more than a decade.

Something about prodding sleeping bears, but he'd made sure to bring a really long stick with him this time.

"Paulo," Carlos called to the captain as he finished a quick skim of the data. "Thoughts?"

"*Dresden* is supposed to be here," the Human officer replied. "With *Mannheim*, those two call Esmer home."

"You suppose we hit them harder than we realized at Vilga's Stand?" Carlos asked.

Nobody had any good intelligence on the topic, operating this deep in Westphalian space and moving as rapidly as they had to get ahead of any reports of impending attacks.

But Paulo just shrugged and smiled. *Admiral's call*, and they both knew it.

There was always the distinct possibility that something had leaked ahead of time, and they had pulled *Dresden* off to one side in hiding. Maybe with a squadron. Have them all set for the fools from Rio to show up and suddenly walk into a trap.

Except that the force down there was pretty tough all by itself. One Heavy. Two Lights. Two GunWalls, one of which looked like it was permanently stationed here as a defensive force.

Without *Ajax*, Carlos might have seriously considered hitting a less important target. He had a list of options, but they were just that: *less important*. Esmer was something of a major sector base, to have launched *Dresden* and the now-captured *Mannheim* at Vilga's Stand the last time.

To hit them back with *Recife* and *Ajax* would be a pretty hard spike in their morning coffee.

Tempting. Oh, so tempting.

"Marie, message to all ships," Carlos said now, loud enough that Paulo and his folks would hear it. "Proceed with attack plan. All ships stand ready to withdraw if this is a trap with the sudden appearance of a hostile force. Remember that we can't win the war today, but if we screw up then they get the momentum back."

She nodded and he leaned back in his chair, letting his tail relax a little. They would need an hour or so to finalize things, followed by a hard jump down into the system. Organize there, and then descend on Esmer like a pack of hungry piranha.

He still owed Westphalia for more than a few things recently.

TWENTY-SEVEN

GRACE

GRACE HAD MOVED out of the cabin she had been sharing with Lazarus, aft to a spot in the Ambassador Suite where Eha was. The woman still didn't have a proper staff. Instead, everybody critical was still on Liberty rather than just being waitstaff for Eha. However, Eha was also used to being her own corporation, since revolution was a thing best kept to the fewest number of people possible.

The two of them rattled around the space designed for thirty, but Grace found that better, as she could control all access. They still went forward to eat with the rest of the old timers and a few of the new officers that had joined the ship from time to time, but Grace wanted Eha safe.

Having just found someone she wanted to change her life to include, she could understand what Eha and Addison had danced around for more than a decade, and none of them wanted to lose that.

"Countdown to first combat jump in roughly forty-five minutes," Kuei announced on the local intercom, mostly just because, unlike previous battles, Grace and Eha had no business being in one of the command spaces.

Lazarus was forward on the main bridge. Addison was aft in the flag bridge, breaking in Humans who had never served under a Churquen officer. They didn't need civilians distracting things.

It was just the two of them.

Grace reached under the couch and pulled out her sitar case as Eha watched, sipping at some fresh green tea. Decaf, because the woman was already wound a little too tight.

"You think music will help?" Eha asked, watching.

"It usually does," Grace smiled, opening things and pulling out her favorite instrument.

The violin had a greater emotional range by itself, as did the saxophone, but both prevented you from singing along, and the Human voice was one of the greatest instruments ever created.

For now, she just strummed the strings, tuning everything just so and letting her hands find the songs that would soothe things.

"What will it take to finally defeat Westphalia?" Eha asked, drawing Grace back from wherever to the present.

They had talked about it, but both were outsiders to the Rio Alliance, even though Grace had been born there and spent her youth training in various dojos and schools before being hired by Eduardo.

One sees very little of grand Human politic in a school, when one is focused on the teachers themselves. Grace had never wanted to grow up and become a teacher like them, finding that those folks all seemed to have lost some spark along the way to the front of the classroom.

Better to be out in the world, doing things. Even if it involved killing people as well as entertaining them.

"Before you arrived, Westphalia had a small edge over the Rio Alliance," Grace replied, drawing on her learning from Yisan, and the times she did go into both other nations to *do things.* "They would have probably gotten big enough to win the war in another century or so. Now, Westphalia is in trouble."

"You think so?" Eha asked. "Both Human nations are far in advance of Innruld Space."

"Ah, but only technologically," Grace said, changing chords now into something a little more bluesy, if one was technically allowed to play the blues on a sitar. "There are few Innruld and many other peoples that could be advanced with new gear, who would in turn wish to sweep away both Innruld and Westphalia at once."

"So Rio needs bodies?"

"Among other things," Grace nodded. "They need people committed to the sorts of ideals that the Rio Alliance embodies, and that's where the Species Underground could help. I've heard Lazarus talk about the need for a grand alliance."

"Will Eduardo really risk all his business with Westphalia over the Species Underground?" Eha asked.

Grace paused to consider.

"Much of Yisan is more northern Hispanic in origin," she replied. "Places that were *América Central* on Earth, rather than *América do Sul*, as forms such a large portion of the Rio Alliance. But Westphalia prides itself on rigid hierarchies invented to enforce a colorism based on the tone of your skin."

"Do Humans get much darker than you, Grace?" Eha asked, coiled now and watching.

She hadn't really had these sorts of conversations before, mostly because it wasn't appropriate. But at the same time, like Oluchi Pryce, Grace Savidge was a representative of Eduardo Martìnez's organization, and the Species needed to understand those distinctions.

"They can get all the way down to an onyx that appears

true black, rather than just being a deep brown that gets called that," Grace said. "After so many centuries in space, there are few people who maintain any true purity of blood, as the ancients might have enforced, but Westphalia contains deep roots of the psychology. To them, generally, Humans with skin like Lazarus might represent the highest expression of their deity's will, flowing down into darker tones. And even then, they would consider the lowest born black Human better than any Gnashiiley or Moah."

"That's stupid," Eha noted.

Grace nodded and changed the tune to something a little more martial now, still not singing, but strumming the chords.

"That is one of the reasons that Lazarus's grandsire emigrated from Earth to Brasilia," Grace told her, in case Lazarus never had. "That elder agreed with you and sought a better life for his family, even though it made Lazarus stand out against the darker hues of the other kids. They taunted him for it when he was young, and attacked him into his teens. At least until he learned to fight back. That skill and his eventual size is what got him into the Navy originally, where they discovered his brains and eventually turned him into an officer."

"And now we come with tens of more species for Westphalia to oppress," Eha nodded.

"The Earthers would turn themselves into Innruld in a heartbeat," Grace agreed. "Extend the existing rigid, species-based hierarchy to include all those newcomers, with the Innruld likely either compromised into the most valued of the non-Humans, or simply wiped out lest they compete."

Eha fell into silence, so Grace began to hum, not ready to turn to lyrics, as it felt like the other woman had merely paused to think, rather than run out of words.

"Circling back, does this battle mean anything?" Eha asked.

Grace shrugged with her eyes and head, even as she continued to play.

"You are here," Grace said. "As are Aileen, Kuei, and Wybert. That makes it the beginning of that alliance that Lazarus needs. But no, this battle hardly matters, other than to keep the war alive and hopefully distract things long enough for Oluchi to come through. He and Eduardo will probably be the ones that win it, although nobody would likely believe my analysis."

"I believe you," Eha replied. "And I agree. From here, I think I need to visit Yisan again and talk to Eduardo, Fernanda, and the others. And yes, eventually, I need to return to Innruld Space to help Oluchi recruit. He'll do all he can, but he's Human, and there are some things that will not transcend species that way."

"Meaning?"

"Meaning that they will not believe him," Eha replied.

Grace nodded and shifted to a martial tune that was one of Lazarus's favorites. They would all need to rally after this.

TWENTY-EIGHT

LAZARUS

LAZARUS STUDIED HIS BRIDGE. Technically, he hadn't needed any more people, but Carlos had insisted, so he had allowed the admiral to transfer one young officer over to handle bridge duties. It had taken Lazarus a while to understand, but Cormac could handle everything himself and didn't need a spot in the sleep and meal rotation.

Still, Lt. Ulisses Lòpez had proven himself to be extremely competent at whatever tasks Lazarus had assigned to the man, and had not balked at taking orders from aliens. Female aliens at that. Or robots. Today, he was manning the Sensors station, along with Cormac.

The NavCrawler thought faster and made fewer mistakes, but that station also handled communications with the other ships, and having the right technical vocabulary immediately at hand mattered. Similarly, Cormac could see what other warships might do in battle, but had to stop and estimate the implications and meaning, whereas a Human naval officer could make huge intuitive leaps based on his training.

Cormac would probably get there in another few years, or major battles, but Lazarus felt better with someone who would better interface with the others. After all, only Marie Oslor had experience with the Species Underground before this.

"Communications, what is our status?" Lazarus asked. That was the real value of putting Lòpez there.

"Signals from the admiral keeping us on count, Captain," Lòpez replied crisply. "All the other squadron vessels will be maneuvering to treat us like another Light Starcruiser when we make this final jump. Gun crews aboard have been complaining that they might get bored with nothing to shoot at."

That latter was said with enough grin that Lazarus knew the young man had talked to Dubaku Afolayan, the Gunner on the ventral Star Lance turret.

"They'll have plenty to do," Wybert cut in. Now-Lt. Commander Wybert of Capantzina. *Fusilier*. "Someone over there will recognize us and we'll be facing a swarm. Your task will be to identify the dangerous ones and feed them to our gun teams and any escorts who can intercept. They'll be coming for us with powerspears out, Lieutenant."

Lazarus suppressed his own grin. Wybert was one hundred percent correct. The Kirov Lance would either cause people to flee madly, or charge to get close. *Ajax* was undergunned for a Light Starcruiser when you got to powerspear-fighting ranges.

"All hands, five minutes to combat," Kuei announced, both ears flopped completely over sideways now in a manner that probably fooled most people.

Lazarus knew better. She was likely to try something a little crazy, merely because she could.

"Kuei," he said just loud enough that her snout came around to look at him with injured innocence.

Again, he wasn't fooled.

"Whatever crazy shit you need to do today, remember

Zhoonarrim Station and tell me what you did afterwards, rather than asking permission first. Got it?"

"Oh, yeah," she muttered with a sudden grin.

Both ears went straight up now, like flags on a breezy day. Her smile turned so evil he wanted to ask for a priest to stand by with holy water, just in case.

Even Wybert flinched a little, but he'd been there when this crazy woman went directly to trans-space *from inside the corridor of the station itself,* rather than getting properly clear first. As she'd told everyone afterwards, she had figured there was a less than five percent chance she ended up slamming *Shiva Zephyr Glaive* into the side of the station and killed them all in the process.

Lazarus smiled at Lòpez, noting just how much of the whites of the man's eyes he could see right now. Technically, the Pilot was supposed to clear all maneuvering with the commander first, or only respond to orders from their captain. But Kuei knew what she was doing. Better than just about any Pilot Lazarus had ever known.

And it would be her tail on the line with the rest of them, so he could trust her to take necessary risks as soon as she saw the need. Every second might count.

Like Wybert had said, shortly everyone would be coming for them, personally.

TWENTY-NINE
ADDISON

ADDISON WAS AFT in the flag bridge. Aileen was on her way to Innruld Space now. That left Addison alone to take over if something happened to the bridge. But he would fight this battle just as he had the others he had accidentally slithered into.

As Second Officer, Aileen was normally supposed to be back at an Auxiliary Control station somewhere, but she'd left Remahle in charge of counting boxes for the newly enlarged crew while she was gone. Battle didn't mean that dinner would be interrupted, just that it was likely to be a Human pasta with sauce and protein, baked in big pans ahead of time and then covered until the crew could be released to eat. Or have it delivered to their stations if this battle went on long enough.

Khyaa'sha would handle that just fine.

At least none of these silly admirals had remembered to put him in command of his own Human warship. Being on the flag bridge just meant he had better screens. Lazarus was always going to be in charge, him and Carlos. Addison figured if he could keep a quiet enough slither, he might just be able to get away safely, too.

Innruld Space. It called to him, but Addison knew that he'd rather be on Liberty, or, Creator forbid, on Brasilia. Wherever his love ended up needing to do her work. He was just a Director who had once owned a broken-down freighter. Not a man who moved systems or empires, and he was fine with that.

Today, he was backstopping Lazarus. Ready to issue commands, just in case.

But Innruld Space kept tugging at him.

Once the Innruld were done, it needed a different name. Addison would find it offensive to remember the overthrown overlords that way. Or in any manner that didn't involve an odoriferous smear of fresh guano he deposited on a grave somewhere.

Alien Space was not much better, because that suggested they were somehow outsiders when it came time to deal with the Rio Alliance and whatever Yisan's commercial empire ended up calling itself.

Commercial Empire. That had ugly connotations, as well. There would be trade, and it would probably be critical that no single planet have to face the Merchant Princes like Eduardo Martìnez or Fernanda Flores alone, so that in turn demanded some sort of treaty binding all those worlds together economically, if not politically.

Crap, when had he turned into a political philosopher?

But Addison knew the answer to that. Too many years carrying those little boxes between stations, intending to slowly wipe out the Innruld over generations, rather than all at once.

There would have to be some sort of Union when he helped destroy those tall bastards. All the worlds unified, after having broken free from their terrible overlords. It wouldn't be like the Rio Alliance, if for no other reason than there were so many species involved, and all of them were generally of the same size. Humans dominated Rio, but they dominated this entire region of space.

Everything on this side of the Phraettis Nebula was functionally Human Space, when you got right down to it. The Gnashiiley, Moah, and Atomarsk numbers were tiny by comparison.

Once you got beyond the Phraettis Nebula, it would be the same way in the other direction, with Humans and the other three rare or non-existent.

"All hands, one minute to combat," Kuei announced, in that typical voice she used to let them know that they'd come out of jump at Aceanx or Dormell.

Just another day in the life of a tramp captain.

Addison wanted to go back there, but knew that it would never be allowed. Eha would be too busy, until all of the worlds beyond the Phraettis Nebula were bound up in an alliance.

Alliance.

Addison was happy that he'd strapped himself into a coil chair designed for a Churquen, or he might have fallen over and looked silly to the Humans around him trying to impress their First Officer with martial competence.

Phraettis Nebula. *Phraettis Alliance?*

Yes, that was what would replace *Innruld Space.*

Now, he just had to go kill a bunch of hard-headed Humans, so he could go kill a bunch of hard-headed Innruld.

And make the galaxy a better place.

THIRTY

LAZARUS

LAZARUS WATCHED the blue-shift fade to nothingness, but he was so keyed up right now that it felt like slow motion as it did. Like those ancient stories of amazing martial artist masters who could actually slow down time.

They'd made one jump from their earlier rendezvous to a spot a light-hour out, still racing ahead of the light-speed arrival of the earlier jump by the scouts. Every jump had to take into account that someone might notice when the signal arrived, so you had a clock started and rings marked on a map.

From an orbital station, all those flashes of light might even look like dozens of ships attacking, if everyone arranged their jumps tight enough together on that wave front. But as usual, the result was one ship jumping three or four times usually.

Or a medium-sized battle fleet today.

They had every ship plotted as of an hour ago, confirmed against earlier plots to make sure nobody had moved. *Warsaw* was right where they'd marked her, but something smelled wrong.

"Target's shields are at full," Lòpez announced. "Engines are putting out a full signature and *Warsaw* is starting to maneuver."

"Somebody saw us coming," Wybert yelled.

"Hit them anyway," Lazarus ordered, his voice overriding. "*Warsaw* is the only threat to *Recife* right now."

"Firing," Wybert announced. "Engineering, maintain fast charging on Kirov until notified. All gun teams engage escorts."

Ajax had come out on a corner, above and behind *Recife* as planned, but Kuei had turned a shade going into that last jump, to slew the bow around and bullseye *Ajax*'s forward weapons array on the only Westphalian Heavy Starcruiser present. *Warsaw*. Other ships were just at the edge of using Star Lances right now, but the Kirov had a tremendous range advantage over anything else in space.

And Wybert was still splitting diamonds with it.

Lazarus watched the solar wind fluoresce between the two ships as the Kirov Lance ignited. *Warsaw* had been alerted, but that was fine. *Gotland* had been caught asleep and gutted, but Wybert had a much better understanding of how to kill ships now than he'd had then. Kuei had just brought them out broadside to the Westphalia command vessel.

Wybert harpooned him. Interestingly, he seemed to slew the shot, bow to stern, so there was an afterimage like a slice of pie in Lazarus's eyes.

"Damage report on the shot?" Lazarus called, unsure what he'd seen, or what had gone wrong.

"Lòpez, you tell him," Wybert barked. "Engineering, where's my power?"

"All generators are on line and synchronized, Fusilier," Lt. Commander Slani called from aft. "Fourteen seconds."

Wybert rotated his head like an owl to look back at Lazarus.

"Next design, can we add a second ring of generators?" he asked, like a kid sending Santa Claus a wish list.

"Sir," Lòpez interrupted. "All lateral shields on *Warsaw* have been damaged between forty and ninety percent."

"I see," he turned back to Wybert. "And your next shot?"

"Opens him like a fish if he doesn't immediately roll away from us and then run so we can't hit that weak side." Wybert grinned by flexing all four mandibles out as far as they would go, and then snapping them back together with a clack, all five eyes blinking when he did.

And he danced a little jig with all ten feet right now. That was almost as disturbing to watch.

"Understood," Lazarus noted. "I'll leave you to it. Comm, what is the admiral saying?"

"He's getting the three Light Starcruisers maneuvered to engage their equivalents, Captain," Lòpez replied. "We have local superiority at both scales."

"Don't forget the GunWalls," Lazarus reminded him. "In fact, Cormac start tracking all GunWall ships and follow them like we did at Vilga's Stand. Feed your conclusions to all three stations."

"*Understood, Lazarus,*" Cormac replied.

Lazarus smiled. This was the opposite of what he had expected, as Cormac had seen two GunWalls like these maneuvering after *Gotland* had been hammered and all their command officers knocked off line. Or killed. He had to remember the CommandWall that Wybert had broken into pieces with a Kirov shot.

This many ships would make it easy for something to slip away from their compatriots, possibly a suicidal move with *Ajax* around, but only if they were in front of him.

Ajax had a serious dearth of guns straight aft that he

needed to address with a future design. And maybe add more generators for Wybert.

As he watched, *Warsaw* brought her bow around, pointed straight at *Ajax*. Safest move, in the sense that it put his heaviest shielding between them, but he just sacrificed all initiative to the Rio squadron.

But panic can be a terrible thing. That single move might have just cost them the rest of the battle, if nobody else made any mistakes that bad going forward.

"Firing," Wybert announced, slamming an upper hand down on the trigger switch for emphasis.

The bolt hammered *Warsaw*'s forward array, but it held.

But now *Recife* was coming into range on *Warsaw*'s flank.

THIRTY-ONE

AILEEN

SHE WASN'T sure about all this *Commodore* shit, but Aileen had to admit that commanding a squadron of six ships, having left two behind at Liberty, was a lot like juggling boxes, back aboard *Shiva Zephyr Glaive*. They were all hanging in space, rather than stacked on squares on a deck somewhere, but the principles were the same. You go here. You are over there, in a bit and down some. You stay on that line until the others are stacked against you.

Crap, one of these days she was going to have to admit that she might be having fun. Lazarus would never let her hear the end of it.

She'd ended up aboard the vessel *S-948* because they had been short a Third Officer after some sort of medical emergency that had put the woman into the base hospital at Brasilia at the wrong moment. *S* apparently stood for Shipper, the way the Rio Alliance Navy did things, like her two Protectors: *P-4282* and *P-4317*.

At least the four Shippers only had Lt. Commanders in charge, so she was a full superior, in addition to being a

Commodore. Commanders Wallace and Aroñezz were on the Protectors, but had apparently been threatened with something called excommunication *after* Court Martial if they screwed up, so Aileen hadn't had any serious issues.

Briston had even fallen in and come along, sleeping in a spare bunk with one of the crew, not quite ready to fool around, even though he was a civilian and she could see something in his eyes when she looked. Maybe when they got to Oton Mari. She could wait to see which way that boy would jump.

The bridge of *S-948* was pretty spacious. Not as big as *Ajax*, but the ship was a long, skinny box filled with smaller long, skinny boxes, so they had lateral space across the beam and had used it to make a wide space, instead of the long space most ships in Rio service that she had seen.

Almost felt like a tugboat in a way, which made sense, considering that it just hauled a lot of things.

She sat in a side station and sipped her coffee. Even decaf was a bit much, and she hadn't figured out how to get Lieutenant Commander Edgar Rodriguez's coffee robot to make anything smaller than a full mug. Instead, she and Edgar had worked out a system. Not as good as her just taking a few sips off any mug Lazarus had, but she'd just dump half of hers into his mug as she went by, add hot water to fill hers back up, then sip slowly at the rest.

Aileen mostly wanted the sugar and fat to go with the heat.

Edgar grinned like he was reading her mind. Or maybe her whiskers. They'd been together for nearly a month now, so maybe the Human was learning.

It had only taken Lazarus a few days, but his life had probably depended on it and Edgar's didn't.

"Where's everybody?" Aileen asked.

"*S-736* and *S-994* are on station," Edgar nodded serenely

as he checked his boards. "Both gunships like herding dogs nearby. Just waiting on *S-1003* to get here."

"It's the newest ship of the six," Aileen groused. "Why do they always have the most troubles?"

Edgar shrugged.

"Somebody had a bright idea when they were getting close to hull number one thousand, so they made some drastic changes in designs," he said. "Turned out to be stupid, because they made the ship fragile, which is about the last thing you want in a Shipper. Makes their jumps about ten percent less accurate than everyone using the older designs. That adds up over this many light-years. But Frieda knows where to go and she'll be along. Not like anybody else could find us here."

"Westphalia knows about Akeley's Passage," Aileen reminded him. "Here in the middle of the nebula, that means bad people could jump out and get us."

"Understood, Commander," he said laconically. "But we're watching for any beacons or evidence of recent passage. Nothing so far. And everybody knows where to meet up if we get separated like this."

She grumbled, but kept her commentary inside. She and Edgar Rodriguez were about as far apart as possible, temperamentally. He was laid back and casual about many things, understanding that cargo was just cargo.

But then, he probably wasn't hauling anything that would get him executed if anybody found it. Aileen had spent years in the shadow of the hangman's noose.

She sipped some more of the coffee and realized how nasty it tasted today. Lazarus had been aboard an experimental warship with a big budget to get supplies. *S-948* was an old Shipper making cargo runs between Rio bases. They didn't rate the good stuff.

Maybe she'd need to buy or steal some tea bushes when

she got back home, so she could bring them aboard whatever ship some admiral put her on next.

"Blueshift detected," one of the crew yelled from behind her.

They were both male, so she wasn't sure which man had spoken.

"*S-1003* confirmed inbound," Jaime said after a moment. "Usual apologies transmitted to the Commodore."

Aileen nodded.

"Send them back a sarcastically-worded invitation to the party and stand everyone down for ten hours so Frieda and her people can get some sleep," Aileen decided. "The war won't be over tomorrow, whatever happens to us here."

She got acknowledgments from all the men and headed down to her cabin.

She'd only been lying a little bit, Aileen decided as she hit the main corridor and started down the steps to the next deck. All the cargo on these ships would absolutely change the course of the war against the Innruld. They had four full Shippers with Star Spears, Star Lances, generators, and shield arrays.

You couldn't build a full warship with them and stand ten minutes against Westphalia, but Lazarus had told her that he expected a swarm of little ships like *Star of Kilri*, each taking potshots at an invading ScoutWall or GunWall from a different angle. With that sort of coverage, those shields around the bow like mushrooms wouldn't help much.

She could scour Innruld Space clean.

Then they could got after those other murderers, the ones like Strav Ardna at Yisan. The ones who had decided that all non-Humans were to be suppressed. Beaten. Maybe raped, from some of the looks she'd gotten. After they'd gone ahead and killed Eha, which had been their original plan.

She'd never told anyone, Lazarus included, because he'd already killed each and every one of them for her and Eha.

But she still had a favor to return.

THIRTY-TWO

CARLOS

CARLOS WATCHED the ebb and flow of the battle, for the first time in his career seated in a place of safety and superiority. *Dutra* had been a lovely longsailor, but didn't belong in any sort of battle.

Recife, however, was queen of the seas here. Of course, it helped that *Warsaw* had gotten badly battered right out of the gate. Worse, the fool in charge over there had turned into the wind instead of running before it, to use an old maritime metaphor.

Instead of maneuvering away from *Ajax*, they had decided to go after Lazarus. Obviously, nobody had thought to remind the admiral over there about the Wolcott Retrograde that Addison had suggested.

So now Lazarus was leading a Heavy Starcruiser around like a big dog tugging at the leash in the park.

"*Recife*, can we go after those two Light Starcruisers right now and leave *Ajax* and *Warsaw* for a bit?" he called, using the ship's name to get Paulo's attention across all the noise.

Captain Quispe turned a confused face this way, brow furrowed and lips shmooshed together.

"Probably, Admiral," he replied "Why?"

"Because I have great faith in Lazarus and his crew," Carlos replied. "Let's hurt those other two now."

"Roger that, Admiral."

Carlos turned away from Paulo as the man started issuing orders to his own crew, centering his attention on Marie instead.

"Let *Ajax* know that they will be on their own for a bit," he said. "With *Warsaw*'s shields that badly battered, I think Lazarus can keep them at bay, backing away like he has been. The closest GunWall will have to accelerate like mad to even matter, and won't be able to get to the rest of us if they do."

"Either way, they're in trouble, sir?" she asked.

"They were in trouble as soon as somebody pulled *Dresden* out of the system, Marie," he nodded. "Without them, I might have tried this even without *Ajax*. Now, I don't think they can stand before us at all, and it becomes a question of whether I can get through this with little enough damage that we can go hit someone else before word gets around."

She nodded and Carlos turned his attention to the crazy maneuvering at hand. *Ajax* backing away and pulling the only enemy Heavy Starcruiser off-line. One GunWall protecting the main station like a porcupine. The other close to the two Light Starcruisers and now caught in their own dilemma.

And two Westphalian Light Starcruisers, facing three Rio **plus** suddenly *Recife*.

For once, he actually had the chance to win a major battle on something other than points. Defending Vilga's Stand and Liberty had been that way, when they got lucky and hammered *Mannheim* into submission, but the rest of the two forces really hadn't suffered any significant damage.

"Admiral, we're ready to come about," Paulo called and

interrupted his calculations. "Enemy GunWall looks like it has been ordered to run over and protect *Warsaw*, rather than remaining here where they might have balanced things out better."

Carlos nodded and turned to Marie.

"Update Lazarus," he ordered her before turning back to the rest of the room and raising his voice. "*Recife, charge!*"

THIRTY-THREE

ADDISON

"HEY, THAT'S ODD," someone said, breaking into Addison's reveries and calling him back to the present tense. He'd been too wrapped up in politics, rather than his part, however small, in a major space battle.

"What is?" Addison asked.

He didn't know this crew as well as he probably should, since all of them were new from Brasilia, after the most recent drydock. All Human, which still felt odd. All still in awe of a Churquen in uniform, to say nothing of holding the rank of Captain over them, and back on the flag bridge where an admiral might normally sit, except that Carlos was aboard *Recife*, knowing that *Ajax* might slip away into the night again.

"I've got a damage control alert aft, sir," the man said, turning a confused face. "The Ambassadorial Suite just lost power, like something has cut a power main, but we haven't taken any damage that far aft."

Addison parsed the words, then felt his tail kink hard and slam into the deck with enough force that it might bruise the metal as much as it was going to do to his own flesh.

It took him a moment to locate the channel he wanted.

"Security, Lam here," Lucas replied immediately.

"Lucas, get back to Eha," Addison ordered the man. "Yourself. Armed. Now. Something is wrong and I have a bad feeling. **Move!**"

Like Addison, it took Lucas a moment to process the words. But then he nodded and rose from his chair, disappearing from the screen without even bothering to shut it off first.

Addison cut the line from this end and opened a second one.

"Bridge. Lazarus."

"It's Addison," he said. "We've just lost power to the Ambassador's frame. Everything, including comms. I've sent Lucas and warned him to take a gun. Thought you should know."

Lazarus seemed to be grinding his teeth. In the background, Addison heard Wybert's bird-voice speak up.

"I should go," the Ilount killer said.

"Man your station, Fusilier!" Lazarus roared loud enough that people on the flag bridge flinched, and not just Addison.

He watched his closest Human friend in the galaxy get control of his emotions and glower at the screen between them like he might cause the mechanism to catch fire with his mind.

"She's got Grace," he said in a cold, deadly voice. "Not sure what Lucas can do, but hopefully you and I are going off half-cocked and it turns out to be nothing more than a fuse controller tripping."

Addison nodded. Neither of them believed it, from the look on Lazarus's face, but they were both in the middle of a major battle, and couldn't go racing off to find out. Even as much as it broke his heart and mind to just calmly coil there and wait.

Lucas was good people, and had been with them almost from the start. Only Grace had been there longer, with the others from Yisan off on their own missions now.

At least Grace was the Human killer Addison would have most wanted handy right now.

THIRTY-FOUR

GRACE

THE LIGHTS and air system fell to nothing, plunging the room into the sort of total darkness that you only got on spaceships that had lost even their emergency lights. Grace found her sitar's case by memory and opened it by touch, slipping the precious instrument in and slamming the case shut as a single, automatic moment. This was supposed to be a calm, quiet moment before the battle, so she had left most of her gear in her bedroom or over by the main hatch, a million light-years away when she needed it right now.

Grace made an instant vow to never be without a weapon in reach, ever again, including naked in the shower. But that was tomorrow, and she had screwed up. Badly.

She memorized where her case was at on the floor and lunged forward to grab Eha off the nest across from her, dragging the Churquen woman close to the couch faster than Eha could even make a sound.

"Stay perfectly silent," Grace whispered into the spot on the side of the head where a Human would have ears.

Eha had a small hole instead, but the internal equipment was close enough to identical.

"Under the couch and remain there until someone you know and trust says otherwise," Grace continued.

Hopefully, she was overreacting, but every time previously that she had been in a situation where the lights went out like this, it had been accompanied by a small earthquake as a generator exploded somewhere, or a beam slammed through shields and ruptured something.

Erlyn had been worried about something happening. Or had an inkling that Westphalia would make a try at Eha herself. Grace shoved snake tail under the couch and exploded into motion, up and away.

Even the emergency lights had failed, which wasn't supposed to be possible. In fact, losing the main power should have triggered a secondary circuit to activate, bringing on various battery-powered lights at knee level specifically to let people maneuver in the dark.

The lack of blowers was significantly disturbing, as that meant that they were completely isolated now, and that the air would start turning stale. At least she had a while, if it was just her and Eha.

And whatever assassin had chosen this battle as cover.

She moved to the sidewall nearby, to the wet bar on silent feet, harking back to the old lessons of walking blindfolded on tissue paper without tearing it or even leaving a mark, every bit of your weight perfectly centered at all times and placed with mechanical precision. Grace dropped into a crouch and let her ears memorize the room again, just as her eyes had done.

She'd done this a few times, blindfolded in the middle of the night when Eha and Adriana slept, so she knew where every piece of furniture was, including her sitar case now. Pity she hadn't previously thought to turn everything off and include a set of night goggles to turn everything green.

There was a flashlight in the wet bar. She opened the

drawer noiselessly and withdrew it, slipping the small tube into her hand like a punching weight more than anything.

If someone wanted darkness, either he would be able to see in it, or was planning on doing something that required darkness. Grace considered poison gas, but that could have been introduced without shutting all the power down.

Even in a major battle, she knew that someone had registered such a massive systems failure, and would be along to inspect it. At the same time, they might not be armed and prepared for assassins.

Grace was always expecting assassins. That was what she did.

But all her weapons were in her room or hidden out of sight in here, and she didn't think she had time to get to them.

A hatch opened and she heard a muted thump as something got tossed onto a carpeted floor, followed a moment later by a hiss.

Damn it.

Next time, she would include full gas masks. A diving helmet would have been useful now, assuming that it was an inhaled poison.

She began a list of places where her professional paranoia had already failed her today and began figuring out where she would hide more things tomorrow, after she killed whoever was insulting her like this.

A quick sniff told her that it was a standard smoke grenade. Probably Rio Navy issue and stolen from an arms locker for this. That made her feel better, as the intruder had probably assumed she had night vision handy and was covering every base by making her blind on top of the confusion.

Grace let the grenade burn and listened for that almost-silent sound as the hatch opened again. It was a room at the back of the suite, with access from the main corridor into the pantry storage where Aileen, or more recently Remahle, had been able to restock the kitchen without intruding in the main suite. Aileen would have stopped in to say hello and see if anybody needed anything, but Remahle wasn't as sociable a creature.

At least not around girls.

Grace wondered if the assassin had any sort of sonar goggles that let him see through the smoke. There was no capsaicin in the smoke, so she wasn't dealing with tear gas.

This looked like someone just trying to sow chaos and confusion, so he could slip in and kill Eha. Probably understood that Grace was a bodyguard, but had no idea how much she had trained in that field.

Grace felt the first footfall as the grenade finally died. The room was pungent with that acrid, chemical taste that you got from commercial dry ice for smoke machines. She squinted and blinked to keep her eyes watering, and then decided to test her foe.

She covered the end of the flashlight as she turned it on, then quickly hurled it overhand into the farthest corner away from where the door had opened, letting it strobe the room wildly like a disco sphere as it flew.

Grace didn't see anything, though, dropping immediately to the floor and moving behind a chair. Not that it would stop beam fire, but it would hide her.

The assassin fired two shots. Once on her sudden movement, a bolt that probably blasted a shallow hole through the linoleum of the dining area and into the steel. The second at the corner where the flashlight landed with a hard rattle, bouncing off wall and then dropping onto an end table, right where she'd placed it in her mind.

Two shots. One gun. Possibly just one assassin, but she

couldn't chance it, or she could throw something directly at the man and charge him, trusting her luck and training.

She moved to her left. Away from Eha. Either there was power in the pantry, or the man had used the manual wheel override to mostly unlock that door before he cut the power, and then used the time after that to get in here.

Grace had to keep Eha alive long enough for help to arrive. If the assassin had a friend, it would have been wiser to keep that second gunner out in the hall where they could fire on anyone coming to the rescue. Wouldn't stop Lucas and his marines, but it would slow them down.

Why would you launch a suicide mission in the middle of a space battle, though?

Grace was stumped, unless they wanted to kill her, capture Eha, and then jump into an escape pod. This suite had several handy, on the logic that they would be civilians and needed more space and time to escape, if something happened.

Yes, that made the most sense.

She reached out a hand and found the coffee table. She touched and then picked up an art book. Fourteen inches tall. Nine wide. Not heavy, but flat, like a dinner plate.

Grace had only a vague impression of darkness within darkness, but she rose enough to hurl the book flat like a disk and then dropped again.

Impact. Something soft that grunted, followed by shots in her direction, but the idiot had assumed that she would stay standing.

Obviously not a professional. You always fired low, because the natural Human instinct was to hit the floor and hide.

Still, she placed the shooter from the sound of the impact and moved again to her left.

Humans are right-handed, ninety percent of the time.

Their normal body flow was from right to left when holding a weapon, so he would have to move against that to track her.

She stopped when some instinct warned her, no more than three feet high, and dropped even lower, pulling everything in close physically as well as emotionally.

The shooter was moving. Towards her.

Grace stopped breathing and pretended that she was another foot stool. Or pile of pillows, since Eha didn't do much in the way of Human furniture.

She could not sense a second Human in the room beyond the assassin. She would have to risk it.

Grace counted to five as the man approached. There was just enough light left over from that flashlight that she could see his shadow, swirling in the smoke. Possibly, he had screwed up by throwing that smoke grenade. Without that, night vision goggles on him would have put her at a severe disadvantage.

She would be prepared next time to flood any room with so much smoke that nobody could see. And maybe add some chemical irritant that she could immunize herself against, just to make it that much worse.

Grace exploded when the man got close enough. Straight out towards him like a sidewinder striking. A fist found his groin and impacted.

Even had he been wearing any sort of codpiece, that blow would have stunned. As it was, he had nothing but pants on.

The sound was the same sort of high-pitched scream that farmers played to draw in coyotes. A wounded and dying rabbit, but nobody ever understood how loud such creatures were until one made a sound.

Then the man collapsed atop her, but it wasn't him moving to grapple. He was the subject of gravity now, and she happened to be between him and the floor.

Grace laid perfectly still with the man on her back, but he was already curling into a small puddle of misery beside her, unable to even whimper yet, as all the air had gone out of his lungs in one explosive jolt.

Hands out, she found his pistol. Rio Navy issue from the feel. Probably stolen from the armory again. Aileen or Lucas would have someone's head when this was all done. Maybe they would join together in righteous indignation to go after someone.

Grace listened.

The air system was still off, so there wasn't even that soft hiss of life support blowers in the background. In the distance, she could feel impacts as the battle outside rage, but she knew that Lazarus had planned well, and supposedly the Rio squadron heavily outnumbered the defenders, so they could approach it with all the emotion of a farmer choosing a chicken for dinner.

She was feeling that way about the creature curled into a ball beside her, finally starting to make noise.

She rolled quickly and struck at his head with the pistol held in her fist, a whip-crack that echoed hard across the room. Any sound right now might draw fire. Blind, but she knew where everything in here was, and Eha was smart enough to remain hidden.

Grace moved away from the silent, fallen figure and stalked.

If there was a second one in here, he was even better at this than she was, and she could only be wrong once.

THIRTY-FIVE

LAZARUS

LAZARUS KEPT that dark spot on his damage control boards in the back of his mind while he tracked one wounded Heavy Starcruiser and a full GunWall of killers coming to rescue it. *Warsaw* had at least not compounded the original mistake by turning away from them right now, where they would expose a wounded flank. As it was, they had barely fired back, probably to keep their forward shields as reinforced as they could possibly get them.

The Kirov Lance was devastating, but it fired slowly. Maybe Wybert was right about the need for more generators next time. Food for thought.

"Kuei, up your speed another tenth," Lazarus ordered, noting that while *Warsaw* was simply slow, there was still most of a GunWall coming quickly.

The last thing he needed was for them to get into optimum gun range and then start hammering away. *Warsaw* would probably be able escape with only her current damage in that case. Sixteen Phalanxes with Star Spears. Four Archers with Star Lances. The CommandWall was hanging back high and away from *Ajax*'s bow, as they should.

"Wybert, after you fire your next shot, charge and hold," Kuei called to her partner. "I have an idea."

Lazarus started to ask, then thought better of it. He'd told her to get crazy if she felt the need.

Apparently, she had.

"Engineering, this is Akeley," Kuei said a moment later.

"Slani," H'Brige replied.

"Start trickle-charging the star drives," Kuei said simply. "I need them in thirty seconds."

Again, Lazarus caught himself from offering an opinion. The woman knew what she was doing, and it might take longer to explain than they had. Even doing something completely insane.

Which just happened to be Kuei Akeley's signature, after all.

He concentrated on the damage control systems instead, to give himself something to do. Lucas was headed aft, with or without marines, depending on his level of trust in the newcomers.

"Lòpez, get me a line to the admiral," Kuei called, bringing Lazarus back to what was going on.

A captain in this sort of situation didn't have much to do. Give his subordinates solid orders and then trust them to execute, having spent months ahead of time training them properly. Wybert sniping away with the biggest cannon on the field, and Dubaku Afolayan and his other two Star Lance Gunnery teams firing at the larger Heavy Starcruiser, while the lesser guns engaged with the closing escorts.

Ajax was backing away and up. Most of Carlos's squadron was left and lower, beating the snot out of the other Light Starcruisers now that these smaller ships had moved to rescue *Warsaw*.

He had the forward shields and spare power to be able to

do this, even as trouble was chomping at the bit to get close enough to be a pain in his ass.

"*Recife*, this is Oslor," Marie came on the line.

"Marie, this is Kuei Akeley, on *Ajax*," the woman said. "Stand by for some extreme silliness on my part, assuming this works."

"What are you doing, *Ajax*?" Marie asked in a voice best described as clinical.

"Something I'm not sure any other vessel in the galaxy besides *Ajax* can even try, Marie," Kuei laughed. "All hands, stand by for jump."

Jump? Seriously, woman? What the hell are you doing?

But Lazarus held his peace. He'd given her permission. If she took him up on it, whose fault was that?

A good captain knew when to shut up. He was trying to be a good captain.

"Wybert, you ready?" Kuei asked.

"Affirmative."

"H'Brige, I'm going to need all the power you've got shortly," Kuei said. "You'll understand why in ten seconds."

"Roger that, Kuei," H'Brige replied.

Lazarus held his breath as he watched Kuei's hand snap out and tap the stardrive controllers.

They leapt.

"Wybert, engage as you bear," Kuei roared as everyone was trying to figure out what had happened. "Gun crews, retarget and fire."

She even sounded like a professionally-trained Rio officer now, but Lazarus knew that she had taken all those training classes and correspondence courses to heart. Because it let her fly the most interesting and possibly fun starship in the universe.

They had just done something as surprising as Addison

asking why *Ajax* didn't bait Westphalia into chasing him, where he could point a big gun at them as he slithered backwards.

Kuei Akeley, already famous for Akeley's Passage, had just jumped diagonally across *Warsaw*'s engagement sphere, like an electron jumping valence shells, so that they were now *behind* the enemy ship, as well as below her, and still moving away.

Every one of the GunWall ships had come even with *Warsaw* in the last few minutes and was now completely out of position, headed the wrong direction and racing at full speed, meaning that they might have to recalculate everything if they wanted to replicate Kuei's jump.

If they even could. Hadn't she said that *Ajax* might be the only ship around that could do this? *Ajax* had just come out of drydock before this. Everything had been tuned as tightly as possible, and *Ajax* had more power than any other ship Lazarus knew as a ratio against mass.

The Kirov Lance suddenly kicked *Warsaw* in a rear flank shield that had no reason to be reinforced. One that Wybert had already slashed at, twenty minutes ago when they first caught the ship broadside.

The shot touched metal. Penetrated. Death by icepick and razor blade.

A cloud of plasma erupted from the bottom rear of the ship where metal turned directly into gas from the intense energies liberated on the alloy hull. Newton got involved at that point, as the expanding wavefront pushed against the rest of the hull, forcing it up and over, like a man on a bicycle that had just caught his front wheel on a pothole.

Except that the rider couldn't catapult over the handlebars, since he was riding inside.

Wybert fired a second shot before the first cloud had

finished erupting, but he was on a different shield facing now as *Warsaw* had already pitched forward nearly seventy degrees from where she'd just been.

If the gravity systems failed right now, people would be inside a car tumbling down an embankment to come to rest upside down at the bottom of the hill. Possibly on fire.

The three Star Lances on the pylons were too far away to meaningfully engage most of the GunWall, so one of them was pounding on *Warsaw* while the other two were suddenly trying to hit the CommandWall vessel close by, itself frantically trying to rotate and get their bow shield around to protect them.

"*Ajax*, this is *Recife*," Carlos Nguema came on the line now. "What the hell just happened?"

"Carlos, this is Lazarus," he said, drawing a heavy breath into his lungs and wondering how soon it would be until other ships figured out how to do the same thing. "I told Kuei to get crazy if she had to. She did."

"Noted, Lazarus," Carlos said. "I will expect a full after-action report that…Shit. Okay. All ships, change of orders. Prepare to move to Engagement Point Seven. More orders shortly."

Lazarus looked at the local screen. *Warsaw* had managed to jump away, possibly so badly wounded that they'd gone whatever random direction they had been facing at that moment. One of the two Light Starcruisers was still around, but like *Warsaw* had been a few moments ago, tumbling on several axes at once. Possibly they had lost power to the stardrives and were trapped here. Maybe already asking for surrender terms.

The one close GunWall had fled as well, but there was one still defending the main orbital station in the distance, roughly ninety degrees of planetary orbit forward from here.

This battle was over, it seemed.

He looked at the dark spot on his damage control boards, worried about Eha and Grace, knowing there was nothing he could do.

THIRTY-SIX

LUCAS

LUCAS LAM MOVED QUICKLY. All his training was geared towards grabbing a team of killers and coming to the rescue, but most of the people around him were strangers to Lucas, sent along by the Bureau of Personnel, and he hadn't had time to vet them all to his satisfaction. Not with some of the rumors folks had whispered in his ear.

On top of everything else, since he'd left *Recife* to escort two alien ambassadors to meet with the High Council of the Rio Alliance itself, his professional standards had gone up. Something kind of embarrassing, even as good as he knew he was. A trained killer who was still only somewhere in the bottom half of the pack, when he was around people like Grace Savidge, Xiuying Bălan, or even Captain Oliveira, the now infamous *Lazarus of Bethany*.

Stone cold killers, all of them. He needed to work even harder to catch up with them.

Grace was aft with Eha. Everyone on this vessel was supposed to be at their action stations, but that still left a lot of space for people to wander around and get into trouble.

Lucas had a stunner in his left hand and an Ares heavy beam pistol in his right.

Lazarus had said more than once that when he had to shoot someone, he wanted them dead before they even started to fall over. Lucas had taken that to heart. Especially today.

He climbed stairs up onto the main deck going two at a time, never taking his eyes off the landing above. Security was down two decks in the ventral pylon, so he got his exercise regularly running up and down these stairs.

Lucas got to the hatch he wanted and paused. If this was an ambush, where would they be?

Pity he hadn't thought to grab a few stun grenades to stuff in his pockets earlier. But who was expecting an assassination in the middle of a space battle?

He would be better prepared next time. Eha and Grace were counting on him.

One elbow banged the hatch control and he moved off to one side, just in case movement drew fire, but nothing happened.

He peeked through and looked both ways.

Solitude.

Out into the passage. Turn left and start moving, remembering to zig and zag randomly on the slidewalk as he raced along.

Lucas keyed open his standard comm and left it listening but dialed the sound all the way down so he wasn't making much noise.

He might need to be sneaking up on a hostile somebody.

The frame hatch was closed when he got there, separating the area where Eha and Grace lived from the forward sections of the ship. He wondered if Engineering could send someone forward from the distant aft, but they didn't have any trained killers handy.

Assuming that this was not Addison's imagination. Still, a useful training exercise he would replicate with his teams to keep everyone on their toes.

And keelstrakes.

Lucas had spent a lot of time studying the architecture of *Ajax*, since it had always had such a small crew that security as a job around here had been kind of irrelevant until today. Access corridor for damage control should be…here.

He holstered the stunner and keyed the hatch.

Nothing.

Not even a beep.

Power had been cut, except that he had power here in the hallway.

"Flag Bridge, this is Lucas Lam," he said quietly, letting the system route his call.

"Wolcott, go ahead."

"I am at a frame that has been disabled in a manner not commensurate with interior damage," Lucas said, unable to help himself from falling into technical jargon now. "Will be accessing secondary corridors and damage control spaces to approach my target."

"Do you require assistance?" Addison asked.

"Negative, Captain," Lucas decided. "Eha has Grace, and we do not know who to trust at this moment, if the worst has happened."

"Understood, Lucas," Addison said. "I'd join you myself but I am required here and Aileen is not aboard. Good luck."

Lucas smiled and knelt down to get to the manual override for the door. Aileen was probably as dangerous as he was up close, where her training against Humans gave her an advantage. He, Xuiying, and Grace were the only people around used to sparring with a Yithadreph.

The wheel turned quickly and the hatch unlocked. Lucas put his weight against it so it would slide far enough, and then slipped a hand into the gap and pulled, careful not to suddenly be standing in the middle of an empty hallway if someone wanted to shoot.

Darkness beyond.

Not good.

He rooted around in a pocket and found a pencil flash that would mount on the end of the Ares. Again, shooting today would be deadly.

He would just have to make sure who he shot. Grace and Eha were easy to identify, and nobody else should be here.

Punishment for dereliction of duty in combat covered having Security marines shoot you to death.

The light reached into the shadows, but nothing was obvious.

He moved slower now, aware that the light made him a target if someone was in there waiting.

"Flag Bridge, power off in the access corridor," he said, loud enough that the comm would pick it up. "Moving inward."

At least if someone shot him now, Addison would know to send Lazarus and Wybert. A powerspear would be useful right now, but he put his faith in the Ares and slid to the left.

Huh?

Lucas paused, then disconnected the light from the gun so he could keep the pistol downrange while he studied the thing he had seen out of the corner of his eye.

Patch panel. Overrides for everything in here, if he remembered his damage control training, so you could cut all power to a damaged section while doing repairs. Nobody wanted to be welding a hot line when someone else made a connection that suddenly turned it on.

He studied the panel. Some traitor had shut down every single breaker individually, then manually flipped the mains as well.

Lucas flipped them all back and then reached out for the big rocker for the main.

"Power was manually turned off at panel A-1185," he said into the comm, reading the numbers. "Restoring now. Alert Security to watch all corridors and flag anyone not at their station to be arrested with force."

He could give that order. The boys and girls he'd left behind would pour out of their barracks and stations with stun rifles if they saw anyone. They'd turn it into a hunt. That was okay. Knock anyone down, so that they could be locked up and interviewed later.

Nobody was supposed to be here but him.

Lucas snapped the top breaker into place. Lights came on around him. He looked down the corridor for movement, but nothing.

He slid forward, ready to kill, but nothing happened.

A hatch was ajar. If he had counted his steps correctly, that should be the back of the Ambassador's kitchen area. A really good place to sneak up on someone.

The air had a hint of smoke grenade.

Lucas suppressed a profanity. Someone had opened the arms locker without his permission. He might pull out all their toenails with pliers when he caught up with them.

Rules of Warfare didn't cover spies, after all. And that assumed Grace hadn't killed them herself.

Lucas approached the open hatch on silent feet and listened.

Nothing.

He moved to the opening and stuck head and gun in, ready to fire.

Nothing.

Pantry storage for dry goods.

He moved deeper into the space, seeing the hatch to the kitchen itself open.

Anyone exiting the suite right now would run into hyped up marines, so he just had to keep himself alive.

But this was the riskiest spot. If the killer was still in there, lights coming on had warned them where he was and they would be watching.

On the other hand, Grace was back here.

He knelt low and put his side against the wall, ready to react to someone rushing him or chucking a grenade in here.

"Security," he yelled loud enough to wake the dead. "Surrender now!"

Hell, they might. Or they might try to kill him.

"Lucas?" Grace called from somewhere beyond.

"Affirmative, ma'am," he called back. "Found where they cut power to your section and restored it. What do you need from me?"

"Is it just you?"

"Just me, ma'am," he said. "Addison is ready to flood everywhere else with marines, but you wouldn't know anyone coming in right now, so I decided to risk it."

"One killer down," Grace said. "Captured. No others that I have been able to find. Nobody got out past you."

"That is correct," he said. "Are you ready for me to step into the open?"

"Go ahead."

He felt like a punk-ass kid on his first obstacle course, but he'd also seem Grace Savidge move and train, so that impression wasn't all that wrong. He could be in the top five percent of the marines he knew, and still look junior varsity next to that woman.

He leaned his head around the hatch and saw the living quarters, but didn't see anyone.

Time to earn your keep, marine.

He stood and followed his Ares. Stepped into the door

and tensed for a shot to hit him in the center of his armor, but nothing slammed him backwards into the bulkhead.

Lucas walked forward and noted a spot burned into the deck. Looked like someone had nearly shot his foot off in surprise.

Nobody was around.

"Grace?" he asked.

"Here," she said.

And she was behind him, but he had no idea how she'd done it. Well, he had a really good idea, but Lucas Lam didn't think stories about people like that were real.

"Where's Eha?" he said.

He was unarmed. She had an Ares, but not pointed at him.

"Over here," she said, stepping close past him, almost like she was unsure whose side he was on and daring him to try to jump her.

Lucas could think of any number of less painful ways to die.

There was a sailor on the deck, bleeding from a pressure cut above his left eye and with his thumbs taped inside his palms, and then his hands taped together.

Okay, that was rude. Damned effective, too. He made a note to have her teach him that trick sometime.

"Eha, it's safe to come out," Grace said.

She'd been under the couch. A Human might not even fit, and would probably be claustrophobic, but Churquen had more flexible frames.

"You okay?" he asked.

"I am now," Eha said, obviously relieved.

Lucas nodded and turned to Grace's prisoner, someone he didn't recognize yet. But that was okay.

Someone was about to have the worst day of his life.

THIRTY-SEVEN

MARIE

MARIE HAD BEEN through one big battle in the nebula, facing off against a ScoutWall in a ship that shouldn't have been able to win. And probably wouldn't have without Lazarus.

Again.

She wondered if the admiral would be pissed at her if she requested a transfer over to *Ajax*. Not that she didn't appreciate being able to ride into battle in a Heavy Starcruiser like *Recife*, but Lazarus might be living a charmed life, and she was just as superstitious as the next sailor. Maybe a little more.

"Orders for the flotilla," Admiral Nguema called to her. "All ships rearrange themselves at point seven and stand by to move to point twenty-nine."

She looked up the chart and noted that her Gnashiiley admiral had added a new place on the map. Well outside of the range of a Star Lance, but just fine if someone wanted to snipe at an orbital platform with that monstrous Kirov Lance.

Marie confirmed everything and transmitted it to the ships around them with text files updated.

"What about that defending GunWall?" she asked.

Marie had gotten all the usual training in naval combat, but fleet actions were a theoretical thing to her. Or had been until yesterday.

"That will be our job, Lieutenant," Captain Quispe spoke up now from her other side. "We've got the mass of iron and cannon to make them give way by main force. All they can do is die in the process and make us take twice as long to get to the station."

Marie shivered a little bit at the lethal tone in the man's voice. She'd only ever been an explorer, longsailing aboard *Dutra* since she'd first gotten her commission. An armed scout, rather than a deadly ship of the line.

Still, everyone moved in a carefully choreographed manner, with the three Light Starcruisers on points of a triangle on the same plane as *Ajax* with *Recife* above and just a little behind, in case one of the other ships that remained took it upon themselves to try the same bounce jump that *Ajax* had just done.

Admiral Nguema had assured her that nobody was supposed to be able to do that, but *Ajax* had proven everybody wrong today, so someone would figure out how. Once they built their own experimental Light Starcruiser with too much power.

She wanted that around her, just as much as she wanted to return to Innruld Space and go exploring. That was why Marie Oslor had joined the Navy, after all. To see the galaxy. Do her six and then figure out if she wanted to stay in the Navy, or find another way.

There were options on Yisan that she had never imagined, either.

Across the way, one big orbital manufacturing platform

floated like an enormous balloon, with a GunWall of ships protecting it.

One GunWall against this squadron of Rio ships, as Captain Quispe had said, was just one of the uglier ways to commit suicide.

"Open me a channel to the station," Admiral Nguema called.

Marie already knew the frequency, so she pinged them now.

"Esmer Machining Platform, this is the Rio Alliance Heavy Starcruiser *Recife*, under command of Admiral Carlos Nguema," she said. "Reply on this channel."

Somewhere, a Westphalian Captain aboard a CommandWall was probably slamming his hand against his desk in frustration, but she hadn't asked for his opinion. And he probably knew what was coming next, just as well as everyone else.

"This is Esmer Platform," a woman came back, with visuals attached. "Administrator Warren commanding."

Marie turned to Carlos and muted her line with a nod. He smiled and opened the visuals at this end.

Admiral Carlos Nguema sounded like a Human name. Somewhere a few generations back someone had changed his Gnashiiley last name for a Human one for exactly that purpose.

Marie watched Administrator Warren blanch in surprise when she realized her fate was in the hands of a kitsune.

"Esmer, this is Admiral Carlos Nguema," he said with a happy growl and his snout perked out just a little bit.

His ears might have been up a little more than normal as well, but Marie supposed he was enjoying this as much as she was. His tail had certainly poofed out in the last few moments.

Administrator Warren seemed frozen.

"I have chased off the vast majority of your defenders," Nguema continued. "What remains is not sufficient to protect you, because those Starcruisers are not coming back without a lot of help. If I have to fight you for control of this system, I will be doing a great deal of damage, including shattering your station and deorbiting the pieces in as messy a manner as I can manage. Am I clear?"

He paused and Marie watched the woman.

Marie would have guessed the Administrator to be in her fifties, with hair dyed auburn but eyebrows still nearly black. Skin around the neck suggested her true age, but the woman had had at least some work done on her face to make it look thirty-five.

Marie hoped she wasn't as vain about her appearance when she was that age.

"You are clear, Admiral," Warren finally replied. "What are your terms?"

"I'm not here to make war on civilians, Administrator," Nguema replied calmly. "This is, however, retribution for twice attacking me at Vilga's Stand in the recent past, so appreciate that I might have taken that a bit personally."

Marie watched the woman gulp. The Admiral's voice had gone from professional to lethal in just one sentence.

"We killed *Gotland*, *Mannheim*, and now *Warsaw*," he continued. "Normally, that would be sufficient, considering all the collateral damage I and my people have inflicted on your Light Starcruisers and GunWalls. But I am not feeling satisfied."

Again, that long pause. Marie wondered if the time spent waiting to hear your fate was worse than actually suffering physical torture. Administrator Warren was finding out for herself right now.

"What are your terms?" the woman finally manage to

repeat, after opening and closing her mouth three times without anything coming out.

"Your station is forfeit," Admiral Nguema declared in a calm voice that reminded Marie of a farmer selecting a chicken for Sunday dinner, back home. "You have six hours to abandon it safely. Your GunWall will withdraw from the system and remain gone for no less than six days. I intend to massively damage your station without shattering or deorbiting it in the process, but if anyone gives me any problems before I depart, I will drop the thing on your capital city intact and let it explode at ground level. The same goes for any warships that get within scanner range of my flotilla in the next six days. Do you have any questions?"

"You're bluffing," Warren snapped angrily.

Marie watched Carlos mute his line and turn to her.

"Lieutenant, have *Ajax* kill the CommandWall," he ordered.

Not *fire* on them. Not even *wound* them.

Kill them.

But she'd seen what it did to *Warsaw*. And seen the records of *Gotland*.

And heard the rumors that Addison Wolcott would have ended Yisan as an inhabited planet had anything happened to Eha Dunham.

She wanted somebody like that in her life. Every woman wanted someone like that in their lives.

She typed a quick message and sent it to Lazarus and Wybert of Capantzina.

Four seconds passed uneventfully. Carlos had not turned his microphone back on.

Ajax struck the enemy CommandWall with a lightning bolt worthy of the gods themselves.

Zero relative motion. Marie suspected that the Ilount

warrior had already lined that shot up, based on reports from the first time *Ajax* had fought at Vilga's Stand.

Forward array and Gunshield weren't of much use in that situation. She wondered if they had cored the ship like an apple, considering how much energy got liberated out the back of the Gunshield.

"Any further questions, Administrator Warren?" Admiral Nguema asked politely. "The next shot passes through your station office."

He could be very polite now. The only command officer left in-system was either dead now or furiously trying to keep what was left of his ship from exploding.

Warren had turned even more white than she had been before, but the woman was a Western Euro or an Anglo, from the bones in her face and the paleness of her skin.

Being Westphalian meant that they believed in an innate, racial and species superiority that should be inflicted on the rest of the galaxy.

Rather like the Innruld.

Marie decided that those folks would be next on Lazarus's list after this, since a raid like this was likely to cause all of Westphalia to spasm in shock. The Rio Alliance hadn't done anything this violent in a long time, trying to just be left alone.

Sometimes bullies wouldn't stop until you bloodied their nose. A small woman like Marie Oslor had learned that lesson firsthand. She smiled at Administrator Warren now like a woman looking forward to teaching her own lessons.

Somebody muted the line at that end because all sound ceased and Warren looked at someone off camera to her right, shaking her head and jabbering angrily in silence.

"Marie, order the GunWall to withdraw immediately," Carlos said. "Same rules as before. Six days ransom on the station and the planet."

She nodded and switched channels on her workstation.

"Westphalia GunWall, this is *Recife*," she announced. "You are ordered to vacate the system immediately under pain of destruction. Your CommandWall may depart if it can, otherwise it falls under the same rules of engagement as the station and will be blown up in six hours with any hands remaining aboard. Admiral Nguema will not negotiate these terms."

She listened, but nobody had anything to say, be it polite, angry, or forlorn.

But then, *Ajax* altered all equations in battle, at least until other people could build ships like it, or upgrade shields sufficient to stand in battle against it.

Captain Oliveira had radically changed the galaxy, even before he'd flown into Innruld Space.

Marie found herself looking forward to the rest of that future.

THIRTY-EIGHT

LAZARUS

LAZARUS SAT at the head of the table and watched the prisoner who had been handcuffed without anyone ever bothering to wipe the blood off of his face. Lazarus had Addison seated on one side of him, bristling with energy to the point that his tail thumps were audible, even inside his cone. Carlos Nguema sat on his other. Lucas Lam stood behind the prisoner and the man's appointed lawyer with a smile an executioner would have been jealous of. Eha and Grace sat to one side of the court room and watched impassively. A few others sat well back as witnesses.

"We have heard the evidence submitted and the testimony of all who would speak," Lazarus began. "This Court pronounces you guilty as charged. As there are three officers of sufficient rank present, this Court is additionally empowered to consider the death penalty for the accused. Does the defendant wish to make a statement prior to hearing his fate?"

He paused there, eyes locked with the man and daring him to beg for mercy. Addison would be adamantly opposed, but Lazarus knew that any information the man was willing to sell to preserve his life would probably be worth more than just another soul sent to hell. Addison wouldn't have gone that deep into the Code of Military Justice.

There was still a spy out there on Brasilia or somewhere that he owed for that very first ambush that had set him on this twisted road.

The prisoner remained stoic. Lazarus nodded. He took a breath to speak, to pronounce the sentence when the man flinched and something changed in his eyes.

Probably the realization that the only Human on the Court would do the deed, along with two *aliens*.

Lazarus paused. Studied the man.

"Lt. Lam, you will clear the courtroom," Lazarus said simply.

Addison flinched. Eha and Grace were shocked. A few crew members who were here as witnesses were shuffled off, leaving only the prisoner, his appointed lawyer, Lucas as bailiff, and the Court itself.

Lazarus watched the prisoner consult the legal counselor that had drawn the short straw today, but the prisoner had needed representation and Lazarus would have been willing to bend over backwards to accommodate both of them, had the man chosen to do anything but sit there and watch morosely.

The lawyer rose and addressed the Court.

"My client would ask for leniency," he said in a quiet voice, probably expecting thunderbolts to chop off his head.

"Your client has been found guilty of one of the highest crimes in the book," Carlos leaned forward now and placed both mitts flat on the table. "Personally, I don't think the proscribed punishment is truly sufficient to cover that, but that's me, and the Gnashiiley have a different approach to these things."

Both of the men over there flinched, even though

nobody would execute the lawyer. He'd actually done as good a job as he could, given the circumstances. Certainly Lazarus intended to put a gold star next to his name in the personnel record after all this was done.

"Does your client have information that he feels might mitigate against an expected sentence of death?" Lazarus asked slowly, just dangling that out there.

Pronouncing it was next, but they hadn't gotten that far. Yet. And Lazarus had always planned to send the prisoner back to Brasilia to be executed. Particularly if the High Council wanted to televise it, that would be fine with him.

"My client would offer what he knows about a larger conspiracy in hopes of a lesser sentence," the lawyer stated. "His were not the actions of a rogue with a specist ax to grind, regardless of how it might seem to outsiders. He was acting under orders, as it were."

Bingo.

Lazarus suppressed the smile that wanted to permanently crease his cheeks.

"You are suggesting that there is a conspiracy within the ranks of the Rio Alliance Navy to assassinate the Churquen Ambassador?" he asked, mostly to put everyone on record. "That your client is part of such a conspiracy and willing to testify against others in hopes that the Court is merciful in response?"

For two years, he had had to deal with everyone else doubting his belief. Addison and his crew had humored Lazarus, but everyone had that secret nod. That maybe he'd imagined it all.

Now, there might be evidence to lay out.

And heads to roll.

"That is exactly what my client is willing to testify to, Your Honors."

Lazarus turned to Addison first, as that man had a rage fit

for the gods right now. But he surprised Lazarus by simply nodding. Carlos was apparently the one feeling a bit more feisty, which surprised Lazarus, but he nodded as well.

"This Court has found you guilty," Lazarus reminded everyone simply. "Rather than determine your punishment, we will adjourn until such time as your client makes a full statement to the Court. If we determine said statement to be sufficient, we will spare your life and let you rot in a small box for all eternity. This Court is Adjourned. Lt. Lucas, you will convey the prisoner and his counsel to a place whereby they can make a complete statement for this Court to review at a later date."

Lazarus rapped his gavel and watched the three men withdraw.

Once they were alone, he rose and gestured the others to join him.

They moved forward along the ship's neck to a room configured as an officer's lounge and found Eha and Grace waiting. Kuei, Wybert, and Cormac were on duty right now, watching over the smoking rubble of the station.

Carlos had given specific orders. During and after the battle, ships that had fled the station like fleas had not been molested. After that, the Kirov Lance had punched precise holes through the core of the station like an icepick, generally leaving the warehousing spaces around the rim intact. But the locals would be months repairing all that damage to the command spaces of the station itself.

The GunWall, minus their dead CommandWall, had fled. That last ship had been abandoned in orbit and broken in half by *Recife*'s main guns. Later, a tug should be able to haul it to a yard for repairs, presumably. If they wanted to.

The Rio Alliance owned the orbital space above Esmer, at least until Westphalia scraped up enough Heavy Starcruisers to drive them off. Except that Lazarus knew that Carlos wasn't staying long. Westphalia would eventually return, and bring with them enough of a fleet to secure local space.

Naval warfare was often a game of moving squadrons around to defend and attack, risking leaving places open so you could strike other places.

But *Ajax* now had cost them two Heavy Starcruisers in repair yards so far and *Recife* had actually captured *Mannheim* and presumably drydocked *Dresden*. That had to hurt, considering how long it took to build ships of that mass and tonnage.

Everyone in the lounge had something to drink based on their metabolism. Lazarus got himself a highball of one of the better whiskeys.

Eha and Addison coiled up together. Grace sat next to him where the warmth of her thigh communicated all manner of things best left unsaid in the present company.

"Did he roll over and sell his superiors?" Eha asked bluntly.

But then, she'd been a spymaster for decades. She knew how it was done.

"He promises to," Addison replied. "For that, I would spare his life. He is just a knife. I want the hand that holds it."

Lazarus nodded.

"I want all the hands," Lazarus added. "Someone had to assign that man to *Ajax* when I got crew members added. I'm sure *Recife* has assassins, as well, in case Eha had stayed over there. It will be like peeling an onion to get to the truth, but we will get there."

Eha fixed him with a cold, reptilian gaze so unlike her normal warmth.

"You get information out of a Churquen spy by plucking out scales individually," she remarked dryly. "Starting with the tip of the tail. They all break eventually."

Lazarus wasn't alone in his shiver.

"I don't think that will be necessary here," he replied. "Mostly, it will be records in computers, leading people one step at a time to someone pulling strings."

He turned to Carlos and grimaced.

"But at the same time, I don't think it is in anyone's best interest if *Ajax* stays where it can be tracked," he continued. "Permission to take an extended scouting patrol, sir?"

"How extended?" Carlos asked with a grin.

"*That* extended," Lazarus replied. "Aileen was taking tools of war to our friends in Innruld Space. Those will help them sweep away the Innruld, but I'd like to see about maybe getting the Species Underground to help us over here. The Yisan squadrons are moving into new positions now, so you don't have to immediately flee back to Liberty. What could we do with ships from Innruld Space?"

"Not Innruld Space," Addison spoke up now, causing all heads to turn his way, Lazarus included.

"Beg pardon?" Lazarus asked.

"I've given it some thought," Addison said, in the manner of a man who had chewed that bone to shards and then licked the shards clean. "What to call *Innruld Space*, now that we intend to end the Innruld as masters of it."

"And?"

"And we should immediately start using a new term to describe what is coming," Addison pronounced. "We shall call it the *Phraettis Alliance*. After the Phraettis Nebula. That's what this has all been about, after all, isn't it? The Alliance of all species for the advancement of everyone."

"Phraettis Alliance?" Lazarus repeated. "I like it."

He turned back to Carlos now. The Admiral would always have the final word.

As long as it was a good one, Lazarus amended himself,

remembering how many offenses he had committed that were worth his own Court Martial.

"Phraettis Alliance," Carlos nodded as well. He turned his attention to Lazarus. "I intend to range across Westphalia's interior from here. As you noted, the Yisan squadrons will help as they reposition, and Admiral Santos has promised me help forward, but it will take all of us to achieve, so you and your friends should go see what kind of help you can recruit, *Lazarus of Bethany*."

Lazarus smiled and let it extend to everyone in the room.

Phraettis Alliance. That was the next stop. Hopefully, it would be the ultimate one.

THIRTY-NINE

AILEEN

AILEEN STUDIED THE PLOT. Counted the five dots when there were supposed to be six. Nodded to Edgar in commiseration that *S-1003* had gotten lost. Again.

"How long until our blueshift is visible down at the station?" she asked, looking around the bridge of *S-948*.

"About two more hours, sir," Jaime replied.

Aileen did the math and shrugged.

"Frieda will be along when she's along," she decided aloud. "Go ahead and drop everyone into the usual inbound lane for Oton Mari, even though they don't have such a thing."

"They've got a big, freaking Security Pyramid right proper close, sir," Jaime noted. "Identifies as *Vigilant* on standard transponder frequencies."

"That means you're in the right place, sailor," Aileen laughed. "The other Pyramid is just icing on your cake."

"And the third one you warned us about?" Edgar asked. "Don't see them anywhere around."

He'd been briefed on everything *Ajax* had done before they'd left this end of space.

"Dunno," Aileen shrugged again. "Maybe they've captured other systems by now and need to patrol. Doubt it got destroyed, since the Innruld don't have any spare ships right now, with a revolution catching fire at their heels. Still, have both Protectors in tighter on the flanks when we drop."

Jaime nodded and went back to what he was doing.

She really was enjoying this. Combat wasn't her thing, but all this was just *Shiva Zephyr Glaive* scaled up about two levels, and she'd been doing that for a decade and change.

Maybe she needed to stay in tan after all? Move over to Cargo Command and make a living?

It was that or go work for Eduardo out of Yisan, but she had a feeling that such a job would end up being at a desk, instead of in a cargo bay.

Sure, *S-948* was mostly desk, but then they'd have to unload everything and stuff. Move crap around. She wasn't supposed to admit to being excited by something like that, so she didn't.

Blueshift.

"We're being hailed by a vessel with a standard transponder," Jaime said with surprise in his voice. "Identifies themselves as *Celestial Sovereign?*"

"Friends," Aileen told him. "Let everyone know that is a Human ship. A yacht out of Yisan originally, but they've been at Liberty and Vilga's Stand more recently. Commodore's compliments and we have news for them when they call. You know, all the usual crap we do."

That got a round of chuckles from the Humans, but Edgar had a good crew. Way less high-strung than *Ajax* or Carlos.

Pretty quick, everything got sorted out and *S-948* got moved to the front of the line for docking. Aileen brought Commanders Wallace and Aroñezz along with her, so Edgar could offload without her in his hair.

Anya met them at the dock and got a hug. It was weird to think of her as a friend, considering where all this had started, but everyone had nice things to say about the woman.

Fast enough, they ended up in a big conference room where any Humans had been forced to make do, probably dragging chairs from their own ships originally because nothing here would have fit them. That brought a smile to Aileen's eyes, just because. The walls were Innruld steel gray, like everywhere, which somehow brought a feeling of homeyness as well.

"You have no idea how happy I am to see you," Oluchi began, once they were all settled.

In any room, that man tended to dominate conversation, but that was okay. Chera Sonels, on one side, had struck her as the quiet type. As did Antonia Veracruz, *Celestial Sovereign*'s director on the other side. Captain. Something. Admiral da Silva actually looked relaxed, which was weird. Anya was all smiles.

On her side of the table, Wallace and Aroñezz were uncomfortably watching the dozen different species sitting around the table, including Tarni, Chuquen, Kr'mari, Necherle, Kreeghal, Dreeni, and Zentra.

The storks stood out.

"Actually, I probably do," Aileen countered with a grin, her whiskers forward and her ears up. "I've got guns, shields, and generators in boxes. Plus one more freighter that's usually four to six hours behind us because of jump issues."

"Four Shippers worth?" Oluchi asked, his voice going nearly silent. Sounded like greed.

"Uh huh."

He turned to Sonels as Aileen watched the man's charisma find a new victim.

"Oton Mari repairs mining ships, right?" he asked. "You

don't build them from scratch, but you've got most of the tools to modify them, if I understand your systems?"

"That is correct," the Tarni woman replied carefully. "What is your intention, Pryce?"

"Aileen, Star Spears for the most part?" he asked, turning back to her.

"And four Star Lances," she nodded. "One on each Shipper since they're big and a little awkward to pack."

"Perfect," he said, then turned back to the Governor. "So most of the ships out there mount twinned Powerbolt turrets at most, not counting the bigger Security Barcs and Pyramids, yes?"

"Yes."

"A Star Spear is an order of magnitude bigger, madam," Oluchi said. "They won't be purpose-built like Barcs, but you'll be able to force Innruld ships to surrender or be destroyed, so you'll get your hands on Barcs as well. Either way, you upgrade your firepower significantly. Maybe not enough to take on Pyramids, but there are far fewer of those running around these days anyway. If we upgrade generators with Rio equipment, and add Rio guns, you'll suddenly own all of Innruld Space that you wish to hold."

Aileen liked the gasps that rippled around the table.

"What about Bajerlie?" a Zentra male asked.

After so much time around H'Brige Slani, the Zentra just weren't as impressive these days. There really was something to say about that tail fan H'Brige had that made this guy look junior varsity without it.

"We'll need to send in armed patrol ships there as soon as we can modify them," Oluchi replied. "Then have Niela Tersand send ships here. This becomes a cascade at that point."

"A what?" the man asked.

"Avalanche," Aileen stepped in, understanding what

Oluchi was alluding to. "Lots of rock and ice coming down the mountainside in an irresistible way."

"Oh," the Zentra noted. Aileen had missed his name in the mess of introductions earlier. She'd get it later if he was from a second captured system. "What about Security Pyramids?"

"The four Star Lances were sent to handle those vessels," Antonia Veracruz spoke up. "That's what we used to kill the Governor at Bajerlie when we blew up his tower."

Aileen hadn't gotten that story yet. Sounded impressive. And she wasn't aware that Eduardo's yacht was that heavily armed. Hell, the two Protectors she had with her weren't that tough.

No more drug running in her life, ever again. Aileen smiled and finally made the leap to full-fledged revolutionary in her mind.

Crap, what if she wanted to stay with Cargo Command, though? Could she convince da Silva or Carlos or even Admiral Santos to build her a cargo-type Light Starcruiser with guns, so she could haul stuff around and still kick any pirate she met in the balls?

Decisions, decisions.

Rod da Silva leaned forward now and speared her with those hard, black eyes.

"What were your orders from home, Commodore?" he said in that formal tone that told Aileen that the man was up to no good.

"Deliver four Shippers here after two to Liberty," she replied automatically. "I have these two Protectors along as escorts, in case we ran into anything, because the Shippers are unarmed."

"And then?" he asked, like a trap closing around somebody's ankle.

Didn't feel like hers. Or it was extremely polite in doing so.

"And then play it by ear," she shrugged. "Nobody knew what the situation was, given the communications lag between points. I've got guns for the locals to use, but I'm not aware of a cargo that needs to be hauled back aboard any of these hulls at present."

"I'm less interested in the Shippers, *Commodore*," da Silva said, emphasizing her rank as the superior officer to Deni Wallace and Juan Aroñezz.

Of course, da Silva outranked everyone in tan.

"Sir?"

"*Celestial Sovereign* is an extremely capable warship," da Silva said. "But Captain Veracruz is somewhat hesitant to send it into harm's way, as one might expect, given that the owner might take offense if I got it destroyed."

Aileen caught a quiet profanity from the woman, only because her ears were forward and pointed at Antonia.

"Do you have orders to return those vessels to Rio Space?" he asked finally.

Aileen felt the trap finally close.

"We do not," Aileen replied. "Pending notification from the senior officer on station. Which I believe would be you?"

"It would, indeed, Commodore," da Silva practically purred.

Then the rascal closed his mouth and leaned back with a smile on his face, in spite of everyone hanging on pins and needles in the sudden silence.

"You are up to no good, Rod," Oluchi spoke up. "Spill."

The admiral gave the appearance of *Innocence Personified* as Aileen watched him. He blinked a few times, as if interrupted at his coffee and morning toast.

"Well, *Ambassadors*," he said, gesturing to the Zentra, as well as Oluchi and Chera Sonels. "It strikes me that having all that firepower is only half the battle fought. Right now, I have two crews of trained sailors that could be thinned some to provide more trainers for Species recruits on other vessels, as well as opening spaces aboard the Protectors for folks to serve on a temporary and voluntary basis in the Rio Alliance Navy. Pending, of course, approval by everyone here."

He turned deadly at that moment, suddenly leaning forward and eyeing everyone at the table like a hungry Sturee.

"While the Rio Alliance is making concerted efforts to support your revolution," he said, gesturing to all the Humans in the room, "you will need to step up and take charge of things. I am an advisor, not a field commander like Commodore Enjehn here. How badly do you wish to see the Innruld broken, my friends?"

Yeah, that was what an ankle trap felt like. And Aileen had a pretty good idea that the only way she was escaping now would be to gnaw her own leg off.

Still, she's signed up for something, and this was better than running drugs.

She turned to her two Human commanders and got their quick nods. Santos had probably threatened their careers if they screwed up here. And then put a Yithadreph in command, to make his point.

And if she turned into a war hero here, hopefully Cargo Command would still take her later.

Aileen leaned forward and put her elbows on the table. She fixed Oluchi with a hard stare she'd learned from Lazarus originally. He was the Ambassador here speaking with Eha's voice, regardless of the other two.

Oluchi Pryce *WAS* the revolution.

"Who do we hit first?" she asked.

FORTY

OLUCHI

OLUCHI HAD FINALLY GOTTEN everyone resolved. Maybe. Hopefully long enough that he could sleep. Aileen's arrival had stirred up a hornet's nest, but in a good way. Chera Sonels had grabbed Sari Tines, the Zentra Ambassador from Bajerlie and begun the process of forming some sort of tentative, multi-system government.

Oluchi had fled all talk of him being involved in planning a government as soon as it came up, headed in the direction of his quarters as if a pack of wolves had found his scent.

Up until now, every cell in the Underground had been isolated from others, following good tradecraft, even on a single station.

But the revolution had broken out. Chera Sonels was now the Governor of Oton Mari station, and possibly the entire system. Niela Tersand had taken charge of Bajerlie. Other worlds were starting to rock like eggs in the process of hatching.

He got to the door of his suite and keyed the lock open.

Anya must have gotten a message from someone, because

she was standing just inside with a glass in one hand.

"I considered being here in nothing but an apron," she said with a grin as he stepped inside and she handed it to him. "But I figured you needed downtime rather than fooling around?"

Oluchi locked the hatch behind him with a secondary code and took a drink. Rum. Or close enough. They didn't drink alcohol in Innruld Space, but had a plant close enough to sugar cane that he'd been able get a rough molasses equivalent.

From there he'd been able to mix in some dried bread yeast and some plumbing equipment and get a pretty good equivalent to rum. Wouldn't ever be a big seller on this side of the nebula, since apparently only Humans drank alcohol, but it took a little of the edge off.

He sighed and took a step forward, wrapping his free hand around Anya's waist and just resting his chin on her shoulder.

"I have good news," she murmured in his ear after a few moments of calm to let the crazy bleed out.

"Newton's Second Law of Thermodynamics," he replied tiredly. "There is no such thing as *good* news."

She just chuckled. Made no sound, but he felt it from the way she was pressed up against him. And holding him up right now.

"So I got approached by some private investors today while you were in one of your various meetings with all those other women in your life," she said with a grin in her voice.

"As if any of them are even in your league," he sighed and squeezed her closer.

"These are bankers," Anya continued when he fell silent. "They have contacts at Dormell and Aceanx and would like to talk about liberating those places rather high on the overall list."

Oluchi leaned back now and studied her face, taking a moment to finish another third of the rum.

"Why there?" he asked, confused. "Oton Mari is nowhere close. That's almost a third of the way around Innruld Space."

"It is," she nodded, and then kissed him on the forehead. "But someone has figured out where Humans come from, and know that there will be a lot of traffic coming out of the nebula over there at some point."

"Okay?"

"They want to work with the only Humans they have handy to figure out how to build Human housing and such. Restaurants to feed tourists. Chandleries to resupply ships making some grand tour. Shipyards building things for the sudden explosion of trade we should expect as prospectors and con artists arrive from the Human side of the nebula.," Anya said. "Even bars selling more than tea. I thought I should consult with my business partner to see if he was interested in forming some manner of Limited Liability Joint Stock Corporation to serve as consultants. And perhaps recruit Humans to run such places, at least until such time as the two cultures better understand each other."

"It's real," Oluchi whispered.

"What is?" Anya asked, pulling back herself enough to study him, her eyes a little crossed in confusion.

Oluchi finished the rum. Not the best he'd ever had, but the first he'd made himself in his spare time. He drew a breath and tried to find the words.

"Revolution is not just a military thing, even though we have a lot of folks on the military side doing things," he tried to explain. "It also has a social component. Folks looking at Humans are seeing themselves as potentially merchants, rather than slaves. Potential partners deciding that maybe they can get rich by working out all those middleman tasks that everyone finds easier to outsource."

"So we're middlemen now?" she asked with a smile.

"Every deal that passes through leaves a percentage in our hands," Oluchi said. "We find things for people for a price. Those people don't have to be Human, either. I could see a cruise line running from here to Yisan and maybe on to Brasilia afterwards. Species Underground folks traveling in their definition of comfort, which will be so much different than us modifying a Rio ship for folks who tend to be shorter and lighter."

"So we need to get involved with a shipyard as well?" she asked, those beautiful eyes suddenly turning shark-like. "Design things for the locals and then see that they get built to standards that Human systems will find acceptable?"

"Those will be the folks with money." Oluchi felt the fire suddenly swell up inside himself as well. "They'll expect creature comforts, and have the ability to pay for them. Walled garden, and all that. A social monopoly dedicated to serving as many different species of folks as we can, with a wing dedicated to Humans for the runs back. You're going to make us rich while I've been busy advising future governments on things."

"Well, currently this is my deal, Pryce." She leaned in to kiss him once. "I'll own fifty-one percent, but if you are interested, I'm sure I can find some way for you to earn your forty-nine percent with some sweat equity. Or something."

He laughed and kissed her. Obviously, the woman had spent too much time around Fernanda. She was starting to sound more like a business tycoon and less like a bureaucrat.

And he'd be fine if she ended up making him a kept man. After all, hadn't that been his life for the last two decades?

Now, he just had to make sure she could keep him in style.

FORTY-ONE

RODERICK

ROD WOKE to a harsh buzzing designed to roust a sleeping bear. It wasn't winter, but he'd had a long day, getting Enjehn's ships organized as part of his own squadron now. Antonia Veracruz had made it clear that she was a civilian, her occasional pirate raids with Pryce notwithstanding.

He killed the alarm and then realized that it wasn't buzzing. His comm was.

"da Silva," he said, rising from his bed with the device against his ear.

"We have a ship in the inbound lane, Admiral," one of the locals replied.

He didn't recognize the voice, or even the species, but he was getting much better with his regional accents. Whoever it was wasn't native to Oton Mari station.

"Go on," he prodded.

"The ship identifies as being from Zhoonarrim station, sir," they said. "And claim that they escaped an attack by what appear to be Westphalian GunWall ships from the description."

Rod felt his stomach freefall.

On the one hand, he'd been expecting this. That was one of the reasons they had gone so far beyond that rim to hit Oton Mari in the first place, because it didn't leave him with an exposed flank where someone could sneak out of the nebula and take a bite.

On the other hand, if they captured Zhoonarrim, they would know about Rio ships operating in the vicinity of Oton Mari by now. Rod figured that Lazarus had put the fear of God into the Innruld everywhere with his raids.

He drew a breath and thought about all the plans that had only been theoretical until now.

"Alert all my people and send a message to the Governor, asking her for an emergency meeting of the Council," Rod said. "Oh, and assume any unidentified vessel that arrives insystem after this is hostile until proven otherwise. That includes firing on them if they refuse to heave to."

He heard the gulp on the other end of the line. That transcended all species, near as he could tell.

"Will do, Admiral."

The line went dead and Rod tossed the comm onto the bed. He wasn't going to be sleeping again for a while. Damned good thing he'd made Lazarus leave behind a lot of coffee for nights like this.

FORTY-TWO

AILEEN

AILEEN WAS in her cabin aboard *S-948*. She'd had to get used to sleeping dry, which was just poor planning on everyone else's part, but something she could live with for now. A rap at the door caught her still awake, trying to meditate her way to sleep.

She rose and opened it, wondering if Briston had finally gotten up the courage, now that they were here, but it was Edgar instead.

"All hell just broke loose," he said as an introduction. "Admiral wants you on the bridge *now*."

Aileen contained her grumbles and followed him, not even bothering with shoes, as they went forward and up. Mostly up, on stairs designed for storks. The crew spaces on a Shipper were wide across the beam, tall, and not that long front to back, with the bridge up top so they had a good view all the way around that didn't rely on screens.

"We're about halfway unloaded at this point," Edgar said as they got to the bridge. "Local stevedores are doing a good enough job, since they don't have the right equipment for standard containers, so we'll be a while getting everyone else done. Frieda at least arrived, right on her usual six hours late."

Aileen nodded. *S-1003* was at least consistent that way. Long term, she'd ask Cargo Command to swap that vessel for something older, just so the group could maintain flight cohesion. Maybe move Frieda and her entire crew to said vessel so Edgar didn't immediately lose friends.

Which of course assumed that she'd be Cargo Command, this time next year.

She grumbled and climbed into the chair that had been modified for a Yithadreph butt and powered it vertical so she could see the screen.

Gallery view, with a lot of faces, about half of the meeting from this afternoon when she'd arrived.

"Two hours ago, a cargo runner out of Zhoonarrim appeared with a message," Rod da Silva began when she got there.

Apparently she'd been the last to arrive. Cargo Command instead of Line, and all that.

"The vessel brought us scan logs of what looks like a full ScoutWall that has transited the Phraettis Nebula and attacked the Pyramid that had been holding Zhoonarrim," he continued. "That vessel fled, badly damaged, to points unknown. The local Species Underground managed to get a message out in the ensuring chaos as Westphalia took charge. They came here, asking for us to do something."

Do something? Against a full ScoutWall?

"Yes, Commodore, a full ScoutWall," he said.

Aileen realized that she'd said that out loud and considered muting herself, except that she was technically the second highest ranking officer here. Her. Crap.

No, wait. da Silva had appointed Quija Yaaksen as a Captain when she took command of *Vigilant*. How did a

Commander temporarily jumped to Commodore compare against a Captain, when both of them were field appointments?

Except that she'd been approved by Admiral Santos, and he outranked everyone.

Double crap.

"Pardon my civilian ignorance," Oluchi spoke up now. "What is a ScoutWall?"

Aileen smiled at Rod. He got to answer this one. She'd been counting boxes last time.

"A much weaker version of a standard GunWall," the man explained.

Aileen watched all the Species Underground people tune in closer. This must have been what it was like for truly primitive folks, when they thought that the gods themselves had gone to war in the skies overhead during a particularly good thunderstorm.

"Weaker?" Oluchi prodded.

"The Phalanx carries the same Star Spear, but only four Powerbolts instead of eight. That gives them space for sensors and a smaller crew to sail farther," he continued. "This version of the Archer pulls everything except the Star Lance and two Powerbolts, so they have the ability to engage things, but again, all those other Powerbolt spaces are now sensors. The CommandWall probably doesn't change much at all. All told, they have the ability to sail a frightening number of vessels through the nebula, fight a battle against a Pyramid, and then take charge of Zhoonarrim while building new facilities."

"Except that they don't know what they can and can't eat," Aileen spoke up, in her unparalleled expertise on all matters *logistical*. "So they will have to test everything and rely on their own supplies until they know what is safe. More likely, they don't ever trust the locals to feed them, and end up with a stupidly long logistic train back into Westphalian Space, thereby inviting every damned pirate in the galaxy to hunt them."

"These are also exceptional electronic warfare platforms, Aileen," Rod said. "That much power can play merry hell with sensors."

"With Rio systems, sure, Admiral," she countered. "Local equipment uses such a radically different architecture and technology that I'm not sure it matters, though it ought to be a big surprise when we hit them. *P-4282* and *P-4317* will be at a disadvantage. Nobody else."

Rod studied her for a long moment. Probably not used to underlings talking sass, but they weren't in the same navy. She'd be Cargo Command if she stayed in. Different chain of command entirely.

Or she'd just return to her vest and capris and call it good. Someone would hire her.

"What can we do to kick them out of Zhoonarrim?" Oluchi asked now. "We've talked about the day when Westphalia came through and started attacking Innruld worlds. That day is here. In six months, I'm certain that we could do all manner of things to chase them off, but again that day is already here. Admiral?"

"*Vigilant* and *Defender* have both been significantly upgraded from the original baseline," Rod said with a growly kind of voice. "*P-4282* and *P-4317* are each better armed than any two ScoutWall Phalanxes. But there will be sixteen Phalanxes and four Archers to engage. A Security Pyramid, even upgraded, is not up to that task."

"So give me an avalanche, Rod," Aileen said before she was even aware the words intended to come out of her mouth. "Two sheep dogs and a whole pack of rabid galumphs to go after them."

"Aileen, are you nuts?" someone asked. Several someones, somehow all in near perfect harmony.

She turned her attention to Governor Sonels and the guy from Bajerlie.

"If we don't kick them out now, they'll be like ticks in our fur forever," she said simply. "Send *Vigilant*, sure, but we'll need everything with guns. It will be just like the last time we fought a ScoutWall with *Dutra* in the nebula."

"Are you certain, Commodore?" Rod asked.

She could see the out he was giving her. Commodore was a courtesy rank, designed entirely to make her the superior officer among a group of peers. If she went to Zhoonarrim, she'd need Wallace and Aroñezz, but they wouldn't be enough. Nor would *Vigilant*. She'd need a whole bunch of little tugboats and freighters with guns, many of whom might be destroyed in the fighting.

But it would be a plague of locusts like Lazarus talked about from his book, if she had enough ships.

At that point, commanding such a fleet would just be a game of shuttling cargo boxes around on the deck of *Shiva Zephyr Glaive*. Or maneuvering all her Shippers and two Protectors on the way to Liberty.

And there was *nobody* better than her at that sort of thing.

Aileen felt the fur on her neck ruffle up as her ears came forward almost as far as her whiskers.

"This is the revolution we've all danced around, Rod," she stated. "That we've all talked about for years or decades or lifetimes. If the Species are going to rule themselves, they have to learn to fight for themselves. You Humans can help, but this is on our shoulders now."

"Very well, Commodore," he said with a respectful nod before his eyes flickered to a different image on the screen. "Governor. Ambassadors. You've heard the offer of the Rio

Navy, in the form of Commodore Aileen Enjehn, to take command of a task force that will sail to Zhoonarrim and engage the Westphalian forces currently holding the system, with the intention of giving battle and routing said invading forces. I think it would be in everyone's interest if you and your senior advisors convened your own meeting separate from this one and determined what you want to do next."

Aileen watched the Zentra ambassador flare his feathers a little, kind of like how Addison always did with his scales when he got knocked off his coil by some something new and weird. The eyes and mandibles on a Tarni face were harder to read, but she'd spent long enough around Khyaa'sha to see the woman scowling and smiling at the same time. Chera Sonels wanted to say yes, but wasn't sure if everyone would answer the call to arms to maybe go get their heads knocked in.

But more than half the faces disappeared, including Oluchi's, which only surprised her in that he was still one of them, having made it abundantly clear that he considered tan a fashion *faux pas* he would never make. Not even if Thadrakho made him an opera cape that was stylish enough for a man like Oluchi Pryce.

"Commodore, at the minimum you will transfer your flag from *S-948* to *P-4282* and prepare for a mission," Admiral da Silva said now. "You will be scouting forward if nothing else, with an eye towards perhaps unleashing piracy in the nebula itself, since you and your friends know that region better than any Humans. I would expect the Akeley's Passage will be fraught with highwaymen soon, if nothing else, though I'm not sure who. Questions?"

She had about a million, but this was not the place to ask them. She'd up and volunteered herself for a suicide mission, when she should have been thinking about taking Briston to the station itself and seducing the boy.

Now, she was going to go be a big, damned hero. Assuming she survived.

Rio ships would be the center of attention if they waded into battle, but she'd need their better systems to try to command something like a horde of angry galumphs. Westphalia would be on her like oil stains on good pants, as soon as she appeared, even assuming a Pyramid in the middle of everything.

Cargo Command sounded better and better, but first she had to save the galaxy.

She shook her head and chuckled.

"Something funny?" Rod asked. It was just four of them on the line now.

"Lazarus is forever charging off to escape his normal responsibilities, sir," Aileen replied. "I'm evading all my normal responsibilities by charging into battle."

"He does what he thinks is right, Commodore," da Silva said seriously. "You're doing the same. I'd go with you, but this needs to be led by a non-Human, for all the political and social reasons."

"Just moving boxes around, Admiral," she nodded.

"That's exactly what most battles are, Aileen," Rod grinned back. "You're better than they are. Remember that. It will all come down to the size of the fleet the local government can scare up to send with you. Tomorrow, we'll know, so go get some sleep and prepare for long days."

He cut the line, so she did as well. Powered her station back down so she could stand.

"Orders, sir?" Edgar asked, from where he'd been quietly listening this whole time.

"Get everyone unloaded and figure out who can get back to Brasilia the fastest with updates, traveling by themselves," she said. "Everyone else will follow as a group."

"You got it," he said, but she was already halfway off the bridge.

It was late, but tomorrow she was leaving this ship, so she headed down to knock on Briston's door and have a chat with the boy right now.

They needed to come to some understandings, and the time for hemming and hawing had ended five minutes ago.

FORTY-THREE

OLUCHI

OLUCHI STUDIED THE YOUNG MAN. Young Yithadreph, anyway. Male. Whatever. He was still getting used to dealing with so many different species that his Interlac got a little complicated trying to sort it all out.

Briston Mara. Aileen's boyfriend, maybe. Something. Certainly he'd gone all the way to Rio Space and back with her, but Oluchi didn't get the impression that they'd gotten intimate on those two flights.

But why he was here was a thing nobody had gotten out of the man.

Oluchi watched the porthole that showed nearby space. Oton Mari the planet wasn't all that interesting, but it provided a nice starscape, with several ships in the near distance and the two Pyramids farther off.

A number of people were here, watching the fleet make preparations to depart, but they'd clustered in odd patterns that were not the same as last week. Anya was talking to Governor Sonels and two beings Oluchi thought were in the shipping business. She caught his glance and smiled at him from across the room.

"Why are you staying behind?" Oluchi asked Briston, turning just enough to make it a conversation rather an observation. "After all the distance you've traveled, I'd think you'd be there for this one."

"She gave me an ultimatum," Briston grumbled.

"Oh?"

He'd known Aileen long enough and well enough to understand that she brought new meaning to the term *hard-headed.*

"Yeah, she told me that if I came with this fleet, even as a stowaway, she'd walk away and never talk to me again," Briston said. "Simple as that. Not take my calls. Burn letters unread. Gone."

"I see," Oluchi nodded. Not exactly Romeo and Juliet, but hopefully they'd get a better ending this way. "Did she give you a reason?"

Briston was silent long enough that Oluchi decided he wouldn't get the story, but then the young man turned this way and looked up at him with an aggrieved scowl.

"She was going to be too crazy busy commanding all the galumphs," he said. "Having me there would be a distraction she did not need on top of everything else."

Oluchi nodded.

"There is a kernel of truth there," he offered carefully. "She's not a commander, normally. Pretty much about as introverted as you can get and be functional, for all she presents as an extrovert when she has to. The woman needs time to recover and recharge away from every other being in the universe. She used to vanish for days on *Ajax,* only appearing at mealtimes, and sometimes not even then."

"Really?" Briston asked, whiskers sideways and ears back now in confused surprise.

Oluchi realized that he could read most alien faces these days, after so much time around them. Probably well enough to make a living at poker here, if he felt the need, but he was never going back to that previous life.

Well, unless he turned into Eduardo one of these days, and hosted tournaments as a way to meet interesting people. There was always that.

"She's shy," Oluchi tried to explain. "Quiet and reserved most of the time. Shocked the hell out of me when she volunteered to go to Zhoonarrim, to tell you the truth."

"But she went and did it," he said.

"Indeed she did," Oluchi agreed. "So you'll need to ask yourself what you plan to do about it when she gets back."

"What if she doesn't?" Briston asked, anguish creeping into his voice now.

"Then you'll have to find a way to move forward," Oluchi said. Honesty was going to be the best thing here. "The past is a painting you cannot change, so you always have it to look at. But she'll be back. Aileen is too much alive for any other answer, so you need to figure out how to make yourself indispensable to her."

"Like you and Anya?" the man asked.

"She's my other half in just about everything," Oluchi nodded. "They sent a spy to seduce me, but ended up doing too good of a job. And then we found that we clicked, so we consciously work every day at the relationship."

"Every day?"

"Too many people assume that things are going fine and lose track of one another," Oluchi explained. "Then things start to drift apart and one day you turn into strangers. Anya and I make time to catch up with one another every day. Even if it is thirty seconds and a quick kiss."

"Aileen doesn't like being kissed."

"Have you tried?" Oluchi asked.

"Well, last night…"

He fell silent, ears and whiskers as far back as they would

go. On a Human, they'd have turned bright red about now, all the way down to their toes.

"Last night?" Oluchi prodded, making sure that nobody else was close enough to overhear everything.

"She knocked on my door and we…"

"Because you'd been too shy to knock on hers, right?" Oluchi asked.

Briston nodded, blushing for a Yithadreph.

"You need to learn to get over yourself, young man," Oluchi said.

He could say that. Briston felt like a man in his early to mid twenties, while Oluchi had crossed forty now and was seeing the first gray hairs come in along his temple, where they would just make him august and more impressive.

"Get over myself?"

"She'll come back," Oluchi informed the man. "You need to start chasing her. And don't stop just because she lets you catch her. Chase after her every day. Or decide that you can't handle a woman like her and make way for somebody that can. Simple as that, really."

Poor kid looked utterly crestfallen. Oluchi could appreciate that. There'd been times when maybe he should have chased harder after certain women, but in the end, Oluchi Pryce hadn't been the kind of guy to settle down and get a job in an office somewhere.

Not unless it was the corner office.

Anya gave him a look from across the way and Oluchi nodded, so she approached.

The woman moved a little sidelong, but that was because she was catching the emotional signature of the conversation.

Oluchi pulled her into a hard kiss that lasted long enough to surprise her. Her arms came up around his back and held it.

"Oh, really, Pryce?" she asked when they finally broke, a twinkle in her eyes.

"Indubitably, Persaud," he replied, with a grin.

Then he shifted her around to a side where they looked joined at the hip, facing Briston.

"Every day," he said to the man.

Briston nodded.

"Yes, I see that," he replied. "So I screwed up?"

"Only in waiting too long to have that conversation," Oluchi said. "You'll have to work twice as hard when she gets back."

"Thank you," he said, and then moved off to think.

"What was all that about?" Anya whispered in his ear.

"Young love." Oluchi turned to boop noses with her. "Aileen had to go knock on his door last night, and then ordered him to remain behind under pain of banishment when she left."

"Really?" Anya asked. "All that time and nothing happened? But I thought we had planned better."

"They are both shy in their own ways," Oluchi sighed. "I needed to prod him into motion a little. He'll make up for it later."

"Or we'll need to find her a better boyfriend," Anya noted.

"I presume you have a list," Oluchi grinned. She grinned back. "Keep it quiet for now. I think we'll finally see some sparks when Aileen returns. And if not, we'll have contingencies in place."

"You are a wicked man, Oluchi Pryce," she chuckled.

"Hey, you knew that when you seduced me, Anya Persaud," he laughed back.

"That was under strict orders from Erlyn," Anya grinned.

"I somehow doubt that the conference room table was

anywhere in her orders." He pulled her into another kiss. "Or the balcony under the stars. Or…"

She kissed him again to get him to shut up, which worked.

"So what trouble have *you* been causing?" he asked a bit later.

"Oh, not much," she said, breaking the hug enough to drag him across the room by one hand. "But I have some bankers I think you should meet…"

FORTY-FOUR

AILEEN

HER FIRST COMBAT command was a simple Protector, but Aileen was also a Commodore with a flotilla now. She couldn't call it a fleet. Fleets were organized things. This was a thing Lazarus had once called a mob, with some sort of rudimentary nervous system, intent on doing bad things once it was awake.

But honestly, it was her two Protectors, one upgraded Pyramid, and a horde of rabid galumphs.

She'd been surprised at the number of ships, mostly cargo runners, that had answered the call once the Species Underground asked. But Oton Mari had always had a bunch of miners around, and those folks knew violence. More rebels had already arrived from Bajerlie, as well as other folks that had quietly snuck away from their bases in other systems, so she was commanding somewhere between seventy and ninety other ships, depending on who had broken down most recently.

Aileen missed Edgar's phlegmatic approach to everything, but at least Frieda's various transit issues had trained her to handle such setbacks with calmness. Commander Deni Wallace was a professional, though, so things were going well. She could park her two Protectors at a spot and then wait for everyone else to show up, moving in small increments since they had a Pyramid to lead, as well as a herd of freighters. Or whatever the right term was.

"Status?" she asked, mostly to break up the monotony of watch.

They had picked out a spot in the middle of nowhere, and it would be several hours before even the fastest trans-space-equipped ship got here.

Deni was on the bridge with her being in charge, and doing a great job of it.

"We have an exceptional map of local space," he said with a smile. "In case anybody needs to land places like this ever again."

He was a tall, skinny Human, with hair a lighter brown than most Rio folks. His face was clean-shaven, but she thought he'd look better with a beard covering half of it, as he was craggy with planes and hard edges everywhere.

"This is where I'd put a pirate base, if I changed professions, Commander," Aileen said with serious eyes and ears. "When we were smugglers, we used to meet about midway through Akeley's Passage, in a system with no name. Just coordinates. The Innruld never found us."

"Smuggling, sir?" Wallace asked, a bit taken aback.

But then, she'd been on Edgar's bridge, swapping sea stories and dirty jokes on the way out here. Wallace and Aroñezz had been on bodyguard duty then.

"When I was Cargomaster on *Shiva Zephyr Glaive*, we frequently transported a narcotic that only affected the Innruld," Aileen nodded. "It induces a form of lethargic euphoria that caused them to mostly just sit around and watch the vid."

"To what purpose, sir?" the man asked.

All the other heads were tilted this way, even if she was only seeing backs or sides. Listening.

"To make them stop breeding," Aileen replied. "Every generation, fewer Innruld, and those that were around were less interested in doing much of everything. Eventually, they would have bred themselves out of existence on most worlds, and either retreated to Innruld itself, or been rotten and fragile enough that we could have started a revolution."

"For how long?" Wallace asked.

"The Species Underground had been active at this project and others for more than a century, Commander," Aileen said. "It would have continued, but for us accidentally meeting Lazarus when he tried to go down with his ship."

"And now?"

"Westphalia is just a speed bump on the highway," Aileen said, loud enough that all the nodding heads nodded again. "We have to break the Innruld, but as Admiral da Silva said, that's a Species Underground job. Right now, you two are the only Human vessels participating in the coming battle as well as the only Humans."

"Will all this be enough?" the man asked.

"We'll find out in a few days, Commander," she smiled sourly. "One way or the other. If it goes badly, we may have to abandon everyone else and run for Admiral Santos or Admiral Nguema to get big enough ships to dislodge our new invaders. But I think we've got enough rage on our side right now, because all these people have had a whiff of freedom, after living their entire lives under an Innruld boot. They don't want to give that up, even for short, weird Innruld like you people."

That got a laugh from the rest of the bridge crew, and a smile from Wallace.

"We'll do you proud, Commodore," he said.

"I'm not worried about you, Commander," Aileen countered. "It's the galumphs that make me nervous."

FORTY-FIVE
AILEEN

AILEEN WATCHED THE GALUMPHS GATHER. Swarm. Whatever it was that this many galumphs did. From her station on *P-4282*, it was a cloud of ships with a giant star in the middle, so she adjusted the view up and out, until it looked more like a bunch of asteroids or maybe planetary rings.

This was the last stop before Zhoonarrim, so she drew a breath and considered what had to happen next. The choreography that would drop everyone into place at the same time, when they would otherwise show up in ragged lines to be chewed up by ugly Humans with big guns.

"Comm, open a channel to all ships," she said, waiting for the light on her screen to go green.

Captain Yaaksen was there, representing *Vigilant*, as was Juan Aroñezz on *P-4317*. The rest were too numerous to have images on her screen, so she just had to hope that everyone was listening now.

"All vessels, this is Commodore Enjehn speaking," she began. "This attack is a matter of logistics as much as anything. Each of you flies through trans-space at a different speed, so we have had to calculate a flight pattern that sends the slowest off first and then feeds in faster ships behind you. I cannot lead you into battle today because the Rio Protectors can step right through, when others of you might take more than an hour to cross this last light-year to Zhoonarrim."

Here she paused and tried to remember the things Lazarus had said, at these various times. Or the Rio training videos that had made her an officer and put her in this mess in the first place.

"We'll be there," she finally said. "I ask you to trust in me and in all your comrades and fellow directors. *Vigilant* will lead, because they move the slowest. Your job is to attack any mushroom that you can get close to, relying on surprise and numbers to overwhelm those specists and chase them back into the nebula. For those of you familiar with the inner workings of the nebula, I expect there to be Westphalian supply ships out there somewhere. If we're lucky, there might even be little stations that you can attack and possibly capture. I promise you that the bankers at Oton Mari and Bajerlie will be happy to buy anything you grab, because there will be friendly Humans coming from the Rio Alliance one of these days and they'll want to buy trophies and food from you."

She sucked a hard breath down and thought about all the people likely to get killed as a result of what was about to happen. Hopefully, they'd take a lot of those Westphalian shits down with them.

Aileen found Quija Yaaksen's face and nodded to her.

"Captain Yaaksen, make your jump when ready," Aileen ordered. "All other vessels will start their jump timers from that moment."

Yaaksen nodded and cut audio at her end, turning to her Pilot to give the orders. Everything over there should be charged and ready, so Aileen watched the line cut and that big box disappear out of the center of the local navigation plot.

"All hands, stand by for your own jumps on your clocks," Aileen said. "Good hunting."

FORTY-SIX

QUIJA

QUIJA TRIED to sit calmly on her bridge as she watched the blue-streaked pearl of trans-space. It raced by in that mesmerizing way it got when you just sat and let the tunnel unfurl in front of you.

"Pilot, what is your countdown?" she asked, mostly to break up the monotony.

Who knew that waiting for battle could be so dull?

Artin Sonez glanced back at her and nodded.

"Three minutes and change," he said, reading off the same spot on his board that she had on hers.

Anything to keep people on their toes.

She'd been through a frightening number of training videos created by the Rio Alliance for senior and command officers of warships. That, more than anything, had brought home to Quija just how violent and dangerous Humans were. Even the nice ones.

Quija had always been the troublesome child, getting into fights as a teen and nearly being thrown out of school more than once. But her aggressive tendencies, even then, paled next to the newcomers. Still, that had gotten her this job. And if Artin and Lamuen Harden—especially Lamuen —were worse, that just let them compete effectively.

"Fusilier, bring all gun teams to combat readiness," Quija ordered, following a checklist created by a frightening Human once upon a time.

"Aye, ma'am," Lamuen replied. Probably was rolling her eyes, but doing so facing away.

Lamuen was the ferocious one. Had she come from a better family, the Innruld might have recruited her as one of their servants, but the woman was from the wrong side of the station in every way. And that made her an exceptional gunner.

"Engineering," Quija said next, opening a channel to the core below.

An Aknaan face appeared on her screen now. Eller Thomir, the man in charge of all those mighty systems, and keeping the old ones working with the newer stuff.

"Thomir, here."

"Bring all generators to full power and stand by to reinforce all shields," Quija ordered.

More checklist.

She wondered if the Humans had reduced it to a mechanical efficiency this way, or maybe they used it to calm their nerves. Certainly, it was bringing her focus to handle the myriad little tasks instead of that dread moment when they dropped out of trans-space and faced an enemy force for the first time.

She'd seen what *Ajax* could do to a Pyramid. Even upgraded, *Vigilant* stood no chance against a Heavy Starcruiser.

Hopefully, a swarm of smaller vessels would arrive right after she did, and then Commodore Enjehn could lead them into battle, but Quija would be facing the full onslaught of whatever the Humans from Westphalia had brought to Zhoonarrim, at least for a little while.

"All hands, stand by for emergence and combat," she announced on the intercom. "Damage Control parties prepare."

There. That was it. The bottom of that checklist. Everyone in their place and waiting for the tunnel to end and *Vigilant* to step into a maelstrom of hostility.

She'd asked for this opportunity, so that she could kill Innruld.

Today, she was going to have to wade through Humans to do it.

Starlight.

"All guns, fire as you bear," Lamuen called as soon as they emerged.

Vigilant wasn't a warship like Humans built them. It was a Pyramid, designed to sit in the middle of a system and fire many turrets in any direction as needed to keep smugglers and pirates from escaping justice. Lamuen only had a few Star Lances, and those were on each corner, with Star Spears and Powerbolts spread around.

Handy, against a swarm. Less so against a GunWall.

"Sensors, what is the local situation?" Quija asked.

They had learned a valuable lesson from Lazarus and Addison Wolcott, and added a NavCrawler named Braige to handle the overwhelming mass of sensor readings for what they expected.

"*Sixteen Westphalian vessels identified by transponder, Captain,*" Braige replied.

"Sixteen?" she asked. "Who are we missing?"

"*One Patrol appears absent, Captain, leaving three and the CommandWall,*" Braige said.

Better.

Bad if they had decided to send a Patrol off scouting for

other systems, since they would find Aceanx and Krahua without much work. But if the Humans spread themselves too thin trying to conquer all Innruld Space, that would make her job easier today.

"Fusilier, give priority targeting to the CommandWall," Quija reminded the angry Churquen woman commanding the gun teams.

Lamuen grunted something that might have been a profanity through clenched teeth, but Quija didn't begrudge the woman. They were all nervous, and Quija had her checklists to keep herself sane.

Mostly sane.

On every screen, those poisonous mushrooms began to turn this direction. Three Star Lances would start to pound on her shields shortly, but that meant that she had extra power, because they had expected a fourth.

In the distance, Zhoonarrim station hung like a pearl against the night sky, the Skycity seemingly undamaged from this distance.

Closer in, all hell broke loose.

FORTY-SEVEN

AILEEN

AILEEN WATCHED the timer running down, like an hourglass that wouldn't empty.

"A thought, Commodore?" Commander Wallace said from his station.

She looked up at the man.

"I've been doing this for a lot longer than you have, and it never gets any easier," Wallace nodded. "You want to be there, throwing yourself between civilians and danger, and you can't always do that. That's one of the personality traits that they look for in this line of work. And why we are who we are."

Aileen processed that like it was an alien language.

She'd been thinking in terms of Cargo Command versus the Line ships, without contemplating that there must be all manner of fine gradations among the combat wing, as well. Scouts like Carlos and Marie. Box-runners like Edgar. Killers like Lazarus.

And Protectors like Deni Wallace and Juan Aroñezz.

Aileen nodded to the man in sudden understanding.

"We're sixty seconds early, Commander," Aileen said. "That's close enough for me. Make your jump."

He smiled and nodded back.

"*P-4317*, we are go," he said, apparently into another line. "All hands, stand by for combat operations."

Aileen felt the smile reach all the way to her toes and the tip of her tail.

Blueshift.

"Wow," someone said, but she couldn't tell if it was here on the bridge, or over one of the open comm lines.

She'd been herding galumphs for a week. Stacking boxes and trying to keep them from tipping over when she turned her back. Anything to keep her cargo deck as full as she could get it and still get to any box she needed with the minimum number of moves on her part, as she got to places like Dormell or Aceanx.

Or Zhoonarrim.

"Protectors, move to engage," Aileen said unnecessarily, but because it was appropriate.

Deni and Juan were already surging forward, Star Spears yelping.

Because of Lazarus and Addison, she had intentionally ordered her two ships to come out low, well below the normal plane of operations that matched the orbital path of the planet nearby.

That put an entire battle in front of her, rather than them trying to thread needles as more than one hundred ships danced in a complicated minuet of death and destruction. Everyone was in front of her now, but to them, she was a shark surfacing from the black water depths.

That was okay. Yithadreph were expert swimmers, and occasionally hunted big creatures who thought they owned the sea.

Like now.

"CommandWall identified," a tech called from the forward end of the bridge. "Routing to all gun teams."

Aileen nodded. Again, Lazarus and Addison had taught her how the Westphalian model, like the Innruld, worked on a rigid, top-down hierarchy of orders. The Phalanx got their orders from the Archer. The Archer listened to the CommandWall. Everyone would listen to a Heavy Starcruiser, but there weren't any here, so that CommandWall was the most valuable hull in existence today. Maybe anywhere on this side of the Nebula.

Vigilant couldn't get to them, as the entire ScoutWall was interposed right now, trying to keep her galumphs from swarming around and under them.

Worse, some Westphalian idiot had sent five ships off somewhere at the wrong instant, so Aileen went from local superiority of force to an overwhelming edge, as long as she could keep all her directors and crazed berserkers lined up and chasing.

This was a battle of morale, not mass. The better discipline of the Westphalians—training as well as inherent belief in species superiority—would let them hold on far longer than the galumphs could. Especially as she saw ships start to come apart under the superior reach and deadliness of Star Spears against Innruld shields. She had to win that first battle, for the minds, before she could own this system.

"Commander, kill that CommandWall," Aileen ordered. "Both vessels charge directly at him as fast as you need. I want that ship broken or destroyed."

Inwardly, she quailed at the words, but right now she was listening to Lazarus in her head. How would he act? What would he do?

Whose throat would that man go after with his bare, blunted teeth, if he didn't have anything else?

She thought of Xiuying, too, which was weird, until

Aileen realized that he had been the one always teaching her to channel her frustration and anger into constructive outlets, both on the dojo floor as well as on this deck.

She needed a sweep. A pint-sized Yithadreph causing one of those stupid storks to tumble on his ass because she was closer to his ankles than he was.

"*P-4317*, put your outer turret into the Archer of Patrol Number Three," Aileen ordered now. "Drift your line closer to him and then fall off our line as we go after their Command Wall."

To an outsider, it probably didn't make a lick of sense. Lazarus included, but Xiuying smiled in her mind and started laughing much the same way he did whenever he talked about Strav Ardna and that punk Khan.

Juan didn't argue or even ask, but she was the Commodore here. Her brains. Her experience. All those damned boxes she had stacked just so.

"*P-4282*, continue to charge," she continued. "Don't worry about overshooting him. Get me on top of that man right now and put everything you have into him on this pass."

More laughter, but it was Lazarus this time, inside her mind, finally seeing that first box start to teeter. It would be three minutes or more before it fell off and possibly cracked somebody's skull.

But she was too good at her logistics. That box would fall on a Westphalian head. And who gave a damn if they were bloody and dying?

Deni started to say something, but stopped himself, so she looked at the commander.

He smiled and nodded, like he had finally seen it.

"Cargo Command," he said simply, like that summed it all up.

But they'd spent a lot of time talking about her past and

his. Her possible futures and his intended path. And how stacking boxes and warships wasn't all that different, at the end of the day.

"Cargo Command," Aileen agreed.

"Sensors, let me know when Patrol Number Three breaks," Deni said now. "Pilot, plot us a path that will punch a hole for all those little cargo runners that will come over the wall when Three loses control of their corner."

Aileen nodded. He'd finally seen what Xiuying had shown her. *P-4317* moving up would cause Patrol Three to rotate to engage the Protector. That meant the galumphs could charge right through the Phalanxes, everybody taking a punch as they went by. None of them could kill a Phalanx, but twenty of them might. Forty of them would.

The CommandWall in front of her was starting to run. Idiot picked the wrong way to do it, too, bringing his Gunshield down to face her and *P-4282*.

Sucker.

"Pilot, execute a hard spin on your gyros and go into full turnover. Give me maximum engines now," Aileen yelled. "Gunners, make do as best you can."

Technically, Deni was supposed to give that order, but that would take too long, and the CommandWall had just screwed up monumentally.

But then, who expected icky aliens to be smarter than galaxy-dominating Humans?

Lemme introduce you losers to the Underground, bubbles.

Yeah, she'd blow right by him before *P-4282* got decelerated to rest relative. And then he'd be right in front of them with no Gunshield in between, when they had the Star Spears and the galumphs had a hailstorm of Powerbolts.

Worse, if he turned, everyone got a flank at point blank range.

Aileen sat back now and watched. This was that moment

in the battle that Lazarus and Carlos had both warned her about, when you couldn't say or do anything. Just trust that it would work out, and that you had the right people.

The ones willing to throw themselves in between civilians and danger.

Protectors.

The CommandWall was taking so much abuse that Aileen thought they might lose their Gunshield in fragments, when the ship suddenly vanished. Gone.

One second on the receiving end of the galumphs, the next empty space.

"Squadron, adjust all fire onto the nearest enemy vessel immediately and give them everything you've got," Aileen yelled into the main comm.

She'd stayed mostly off of the line up until now. The galumphs that were here were the ones willing to go after storks, and there were too many of them to do more than occasionally offer suggestions. But with the Human commander fleeing, the rest would as soon as they could charge their stardrives.

And they couldn't reinforce shields and charge capacitors at the same time. Only *Ajax* could do that.

Ninety seconds of hell, and orbital space above Zhoonarrim was empty of Westphalian ships.

No kills, but scanners suggested more than half of the fleeing Westphalian ships were ready for drydock, assuming that they could get home from here. Maybe a few for the scrap yard.

There was no place in Innruld Space safe for them.

"Congratulations, Commodore," Deni beamed.

"I'm not done yet," Aileen growled as she typed.

The man's face fell into confusion, but he was Line, and she was Cargo Command.

That also included piracy.

"*Vigilant*, this is Aileen," she said, still talking over the big comm so all the directors in the system could hear her, including the station folks and any Humans suddenly left without a ride.

"Go ahead, Commodore," Quija replied.

Vigilant had gotten pounded, but only briefly, because the galumphs had showed up and turned this into a mud wrestling match.

"Captain Yaaksen, you will take command of local space and supervise the surrender of Zhoonarrim Station to the Species Underground," Aileen ordered. "For everyone else, I am transmitting a series of locations that are the most likely stopping points for an enemy force attempting to flee into the nebula ahead of us. I will remind you that they can jump straight and fast, but cannot turn corners in trans-space like we do. Plus, they're hurt and just got their tails singed."

Well, they didn't have tails, but most of the Species did, and they'd understand a little literary license here.

"I am ordering any ships following to commit random acts of piracy against any Westphalian vessel they encounter in the Nebula," Aileen ordered. "However, look before you shoot, because I am also expecting vessels from Yisan, like our friend *Celestial Sovereign*, as well as more cargo and ships of the line from the Rio Alliance. Both of those are our allies, so if you find them, there will be rewards for helping them get to Zhoonarrim, Oton Mari, or Bajerlie."

She paused and caught Deni's smile from across his bridge.

"Protector squadron, make your first jump," Aileen ordered.

FORTY-EIGHT
AILEEN

IT HAD NEARLY BEEN a suicidal mistake on her part, but one Aileen was willing to make. Looking around as they blueshifted just to the edge of the system, the Westphalian squadron was scattered all to hell, with signals from all directions, some of them as much as two light-hours out.

But then, they'd run like hell without their CommandWall issuing those sorts of careful, box-stacking orders that kept cargo decks and fleet operations clean.

"Engage the nearest ship, priority to anything showing visible damage," Aileen ordered as the scanners started making sense of enemy targets. "Stay together and trickle-charge your stardrives for when we need to run."

Deni grunted something and Aileen went back to being a commodore.

There had been sixteen enemy ships at Zhoonarrim. Jumping right into their midst now was the highest folly, but they were panicked, wounded, and running for their lives, so two Protectors could chivy them along.

Anything was better than letting them get organized and

decide that maybe they could return the favor at Zhoonarrim.

P-4282 had an Archer close enough to engage. Pure luck, but it had been a part of Patrol Three, and had already gotten the angry end of a lot of fists. *P-4317* stayed tight on their wing and both opened fire.

This was that moment when the design of a turret on either wing worked in their favor. GunWall ships could maneuver, but that Star Lance was on the centerline of the ship, so they had to turn radically to bring to bear against someone popping out of hyperspace on their flank.

Around her, the rest of the force was scattered and starting to move this direction, which would be a problem soon, because all their guns would be facing inwards when they did.

But like *Vigilant*, hopefully, she only had to hold the center for a little while.

"Target has struck his colors," Deni yelled loud enough that everyone registered. "Aileen, he's surrendering."

"Move on to the next target," she ordered grimly.

Assuming that Westphalia would honor their own rules, that meant he would stop fighting and wait meekly for *aliens* to come aboard and take charge. Wouldn't be her, for all the obvious reasons, but she would probably send someone from her Protectors, if only to limit the amount of hostility that would erupt if they suddenly had to answer to a Kreeghal or something.

And if he fired again, having surrendered, Aileen was within her rights to just blast him out of existence and shoot every lifepod emerging from his hull as she did.

Human rules were weird, but they'd been doing armed mayhem professionally for a long time. And some idiot had commissioned her as a Commander in the Rio Alliance Navy. And then another idiot had put her in charge here.

There was a Phalanx moving to engage now, bow on and everything firing. But this was just the opposite of the last battle, where she'd had to stack her boxes and galumphs precisely, to get everyone there at the same time.

One Phalanx was not a match for two Protectors. Other than he would continue to wear things down that the Archer and the previous battle had damaged.

Death by attrition, or a thousand paper cuts, but Aileen was prepared to run before that happened.

"Engaging target eleven," Deni said, but she wasn't paying that close of attention.

She had dialed her scanner back to show a span of ten light-minutes now. More than half of the Westphalian ships were within that, but only half, so they would be jumping headlong to the rescue now, once the light signal reached them that this was not a safe harbor in which to hide.

She was racing against another clock.

A second Phalanx came out of jump nearby. Different flank. Possibly intentionally, but maybe just the luck of the draw that had them bracketing. *P-4317* immediately pivoted their attention to the newcomer.

Lazarus had said that two Protectors could handle three Gun Phalanxes, but that a full GunWall Patrol would probably win. This was a lesser being. A ScoutWall. Assuming fresh ships, fresh crews, and time to maneuver, they might still need five ships fighting as a unit. This mess was anything but organized.

And then the first ping appeared on her screen and Aileen felt a weight slide off her back and land perfectly where she had intended the next box to rest in shipping.

"Friendly vessels emerging from jump," Deni called, unnecessarily to her, but maybe to remind all the gunners on both ships that they weren't alone. "Moving to engage. All vessels, target number twelve has surrendered to us. Do not fire on them."

Protectors leapt to interpose themselves between civilians and danger. That was the job. But sometimes the civilians came to your rescue as well.

Five signals. Six. Eight. Eleven. Seventeen.

She had a pack of galumphs again. The skies on her board showed it raining Powerbolts in every direction, but the Phalanxes were inside a shell now, taking fire on weak flanks that didn't have a Gunshield to interpose.

More were coming every moment, as trans-space drives moved everyone at a different speed and this had been a short jump out to the edge of the Zhoonarrim system. That safe spot where you figured out which star you were approaching before jumping down into the warm spots to trade.

Or fight.

One of the two Phalanxes nearby and still fighting suddenly vanished. The other struck his colors.

Shit, was it possible to actually capture these people?

Aileen had been expecting those specist punks to fight to the death against things with fur, scales, or feathers.

Around her, she watched Westphalian signals vanish as they realized that they'd only partly escaped, and that now they had to truly run for their lives.

"All Species Underground vessels attention," Aileen said on her command channel. "I will take charge of these two vessels as you chase the others deeper into the nebula. *P-4317*, you will take tactical command of those operations, but don't go more than four or five more jumps deeper in for now. Just harry them. Damage them when you can. Break up their concentrations and make them flee in solitude. Get them to surrender and bring them back to me here."

Crap, now she was sounding like Lazarus when she gave

orders. But he was a pretty good person to learn from. And she had just won her first space fleet battle. Really won.

Chasing the Humans off from Zhoonarrim had always been an expected outcome, once she knew how many galumphs had answered that call. But catching them here and chasing them like pack predators was a whole different thing.

Leave Innruld Space and never come back!

Not that she could enforce such an order, but when these Humans got home and told everyone that they'd been set upon by an angry mob…

Better, when not all of them made it home…

Aileen sucked a hard breath deep into her stomach to try to break up that ball of cold that had taken root. She might actually drink all of a mug of decaf coffee right now, just for the heat and fat she would add.

She turned to Deni and smiled grimly.

"I will need two officers and two crew members for those prize vessels," she said simply. "They should be Human, and be under orders to behave themselves like this was a Rio Alliance operation, because we are under the orders of Admiral da Silva."

Then she relented a little and smiled.

"But let the folks over there know if they get snippy that I could have invaded them with Churquen, Yithadreph, Dreeni, Aknaan, or something really weird if I had wanted to. And might, if they give me any trouble before I find a ship to send them home."

"Home?" Deni asked carefully.

"Home, Commander," Aileen said. "We are not savages. You are the Rio Alliance Navy, under command of a Rio Commodore. You will do this by the book, from introduction to appendix. Questions?"

"No, sir," he said sharply, shoulders snapping back unconsciously, if she had to guess.

"Good," she said. "Take charge and make sure that all new vessels arriving to help get routed off after Juan."

"Will do, Commodore."

Aileen headed over to the coffee robot and dialed her needs in. Deni got a slightly better cut of coffee than Edgar had, but it would still be nasty and bitter, even after adding as much sugar and cream as she could.

But it was what she needed right now.

FORTY-NINE

LAZARUS

LAZARUS WATCHED the vessels come out of jump at the far end of the Inbound Lane as *Vigilant* was enforcing it today.

"*Alert,*" Cormac chirped. "*Two enemy GunWall vessels…*"

It was weird, hearing a NavCrawler falter in the middle of a sentence. Lazarus wasn't sure he'd ever actually heard Cormac at a loss for words before.

"*Lazarus, both vessels are flying Rio transponder codes,*" Cormac continued. "*Ah. P-4282 has arrived with them and is transmitting an update. These vessels have been captured.*"

Lazarus had guessed that as soon as they had arrived at Zhoonarrim, as they were flying like Rio ships. And two against this system would have been suicide, even before *Ajax* and his support squadron had arrived.

Carlos had let him bring *PL-371* and her consorts, *P-4491* and *P-4502*. Rod da Silva was practically salivating with the opportunities at hand.

"Hail them and send my compliments to the Commodore," Lazarus said.

He turned to Addison and smiled.

Eha was a little more nervous, coiled and twined with her mate. He would have said green around the gills, but green was her normal status.

"What do we do with GunWall ships?" Addison asked.

They had only been in-system long enough to take in the situation, a day after the battle, in spite of the corners Kuei had cut to get them here from Oton Mari after that long sail from Rio space over the top of the nebula.

Eha interrupted before Lazarus could speak.

"We turn them into the start of our new navy," she said simply. "Plus any others that trickle in. Even a Phalanx is better than anything in our alliance against a Pyramid. Is that one an Archer?"

"*It is, Ambassador,*" Cormac replied.

"Then we have begun," Eha said.

"Begun?" Lazarus asked, a bit confused, but she'd gone to a different headspace since the assassination attempt. More serious. She reminded him of Erlyn Teixeira more and more each day, but that was appropriate. She would sit on the High Council, one of these days. At least until she decided she didn't want to.

"As Addison said," Eha nodded to him. "The Phraettis Alliance needs to meet Yisan and Rio on equal footing. If we can field a navy to your standards, then we are on our way."

She paused there, but Lazarus let the silence stretch. This woman was up to something.

"How long would it take to train Phraettis Alliance crews to fly those ships?" she asked him now. "To take them into combat as part of a Rio force, attacking Westphalian systems?"

"If I pull a training cadre of folks off our ships, we can start the process immediately," Lazarus said. "I finally have enough crew members at this end of the galaxy to do something like that. Aileen does as well, with her two

Protectors. Getting your trainees to our standards might take as much as a year, but that's just learning the intricacies of the technology. You'll have a mob of volunteers who are all experienced sailors. And they just won a major battle. That goes a long ways."

"Good," she said. "Let's all convene on *Vigilant*, then, and have a chat."

Lazarus could see the machinations churning in that woman's eyes at the word *chat*. If he was an enemy, he'd be frightened.

But she was the Phraettis Alliance. And that chat would be how to take the war to Westphalia, for the future of the galaxy itself.

FIFTY

LAZARUS

THEY WERE all in a welcoming line for the conquering hero. Lazarus was last, both because he hadn't been here, and because he'd put his foot down and told Quija she should have the place of honor at the front.

Aileen came through the bay door, with Commander Wallace trailing her by a step. She looked good in tan, but he could see where Thadrakho would need to take in her uniform.

The stress of command frequently caused him to lose weight, so he already understood.

She greeted everyone and got lionized as a total badass, which made her blush, visible even over here as he watched her ears and whiskers move.

Finally, she got all the way down to him. Paused, looking up at him. Threw herself into a great big hug.

"I'm not sure it is entirely appropriate for a superior officer to hug people," he said wryly.

"Don't make me tickle you," she growled back.

"Ah," he chuckled, holding her close and talking quietly.

"I was afraid someone needed her back scratched in the shower or something."

"That's coming," she murmured. "You or Grace. Both have adequate nails for the task."

He finally felt her lean back.

"That was the worst thing I have ever done," Aileen said as she finally untangled herself and stepped back, careful not to tread on anyone's toes or tail as they all crowded around her now.

"I know," Lazarus acknowledged. "The only thing worse is losing. I've been there, too. But it brought me here, so I always count that as a silver lining. What are you doing with your prisoners?"

"I need to send someone to Oton Mari and have my Shippers reroute this direction," she replied, sounding like a command officer, in spite of how much he knew she hated that sort of thing.

Or did she? This was a different woman, just as Eha had changed recently.

Hopefully Grace wasn't about to turn into someone else on him. Lazarus wasn't sure who he'd have to become to keep that woman happy.

"I will send them home on those hulls, with a lot of food and cargo, both Protectors, and whoever else wants to convoy that direction," Aileen said.

"You should probably accompany them personally, Commodore," Lazarus reminded her.

Technically, she outranked him and Addison, but he knew how much she would rather chuck it all and go back to moving boxes around.

"Oh, it's worse than that, *Captain*," she replied, with a sudden, evil twinkle in her eyes. She paused to look at Addison as well. "*Captains*. You'll be accompanying me.

We've pushed them out of Zhoonarrim. I want them out of my nebula, as well."

"Your nebula, Aileen?" Lazarus asked.

"Mine," she nodded. "My galumphs are currently out there with Juan, chasing down the rest and either forcing them to surrender, or driving them like *wahqfs* until they manage to outrun us to the Human side. I've also ordered them to attack any Westphalian vessel or station they find, or bring me back the coordinates so we can haul *Vigilant* or *Ajax* out there to do the job. Yisan and Rio hulls are to be escorted here as rapidly as possible."

"Your nebula, then," Lazarus nodded.

He hugged her again, just because. Other hands reached in to touch and to welcome her home.

It should be her nebula. Fitting, since it had all started there when he'd turned *Ajax* on a collision course with whatever star he slammed into, and disappeared into the depths.

Now, the Phraettis Alliance would emerge from those same clouds.

And the galaxy would never be the same.

READ MORE

Be sure to read all the books in the Lazarus Alliance series!

Escape
Return
Rebellion
Revolution
Liberation
Retribution
Alliance

Available at your favorite retailers!

ABOUT THE AUTHOR

Blaze Ward writes science fiction in the Alexandria Station universe (Jessica Keller, The Science Officer, The Story Road, etc.) as well as several other science fiction universes, such as Star Dragon, the Dominion, and more. He also writes odd bits of high fantasy with swords and orcs. In addition, he is the Editor and Publisher of *Boundary Shock Quarterly Magazine*. You can find out more at his website www.blazeward.com, as well as Facebook, Goodreads, and other places.

Blaze's works are available as ebooks, paper, and audio, and can be found at a variety of online vendors. His newsletter comes out regularly, and you can also follow his blog on his website. He really enjoys interacting with fans, and looks forward to any and all questions—even ones about his books!

Never miss a release!
If you'd like to be notified of new releases, sign up for my newsletter.

http://www.blazeward.com/newsletter/

Buy More!
Did you know that you can buy directly from my website?

https://www.blazeward.com/shop/

Connect with Blaze!

Web: www.blazeward.com
Boundary Shock Quarterly (BSQ):
https://www.boundaryshockquarterly.com/

ABOUT KNOTTED ROAD PRESS

Knotted Road Press fiction specializes in dynamic writing set in mysterious, exotic locations.

Knotted Road Press non–fiction publishes autobiographies, business books, cookbooks, and how–to books with unique voices.

Knotted Road Press creates DRM–free ebooks as well as high–quality print books for readers around the world.

With authors in a variety of genres including literary, poetry, mystery, fantasy, and science fiction, Knotted Road Press has something for everyone.

Knotted Road Press
www.KnottedRoadPress.com